SECOND
CHANCES

PAGE PUBLISHING, INC.
Conneaut Lake, PA

First originally published by Page Publishing 2019

ISBN 978-1-64628-680-5 (pbk)
ISBN 978-1-64628-681-2 (digital)

Printed in the United States of America

Second Chances

A. S. McConnell

Dedication

To my family, husband, and children. Thank you for always believing in me. You are my purpose and love of life. My ambition is endless because of your love and support.

Being deeply loved by someone gives you strength, while loving someone deeply gives you courage.

—Lao Tzu

SECOND CHANCES

1

As Ava Stillman looked out her glass-walled, high-rise apartment at the city of New York, she felt the warmth of a new day upon her face as the sun began to rise. She tucked a strand of her dark-blond hair behind her ear as she sipped her morning coffee, a comforting routine which always gave her the feeling of home—a place where each day laid forth a set of new possibilities and a sense of calm.

She might currently live in the city, but Ava was a country girl at heart. Growing up in a rural community afforded Ava the opportunity to enjoy the friendliness of a small town where everyone knew your name and genuinely cared about your well-being.

Ava inhaled her vanilla french roast coffee and could almost see her mom in the kitchen, brewing up a batch for her Dad. He would be getting ready to head out the door for work, but no matter the day, he would always find a way to sneak in a kiss on her mother's cheek before leaving the house.

Her parents had been married for decades, and he still managed to make it seem like they had just met and fallen in love. Ava's notion of a great relationship was modeled after her parents' devotion to one another.

It was difficult to believe her dad had passed away nearly three years ago. She missed him deeply, especially on the days when she needed advice. His hearty laugh could make her smile in any situation, and his knowing when something was wrong even before Ava said anything, somehow made telling him things easier.

The sun began to break through the clouds, making the city lights fade. Ava cherished the mornings when she could be alone with her thoughts. She soaked in the stillness of the streets before they began to fill with tourists and professionals hurrying to work.

Turning away from the window and exhaling softly, Ava quietly walked back to her bedroom to find her boyfriend, Eric Gallops, of a year sleeping peacefully. He was a foot taller than her and towered over her as a protector, which Ava sought after in a companion.

Eric's dark features complemented his sense of mystery and seduction. His eyes were captivating, and his well-toned physic often made women stare whenever they were out, but he always knew how to make Ava feel special.

Lately, however, he seemed preoccupied, but Ava attributed his uncharacteristic behavior to a potential question he was looking to ask her on their upcoming vacation next month.

They had planned a long weekend away to the Bahamas. Sun and relaxation were exactly what they both needed. Their professions took many days and some nights away from each other, so an uninterrupted getaway was the perfect gift for each other.

Ava thought for a moment about Eric asking her to marry him and what it would mean to be someone's wife. She secretly hoped to find a love as deep and true as her parents. She quietly entertained the notion as she gazed at him from the doorway.

As Ava began to think of marrying Eric, the memories of her first love, Calvin William Michaels, came flooding into her mind. She quickly shook the idea—of what could have been between them had she not gone away to school—out of her head. Their relationship ended nearly ten years ago, and she refused to think of Cal when Eric might be proposing soon.

Remembering she had an important meeting this morning for work, Ava quietly stepped into the bathroom to get ready for her day. As she showered, she took a moment to think about the type of wedding she would want, where they would get married, and how soon Eric would want children.

Growing up, Ava had always wanted three kids. When she was with Cal, they talked about wanting a big family and what they would name their children. Eric wasn't necessarily forthcoming in how many he wanted, but he usually made a comment that having a child would allow him to carry on his family name.

Ava stepped out of the shower, put on her white satin robe, and looked at herself in the mirror, thinking, *Yes, I can do this. I could be Mrs. Eric Gallops.*

She smiled brightly at her reflection, and with a sense of giddiness, she made her way to the walk-in closet to choose an outfit that would make a powerful and assertive statement for her big meeting today.

The meeting was important not only to her company but for her reputation as well. Ava had single-handedly landed the client and worked effortlessly for months negotiating their contracts.

Ava's diplomacy was well-known around the office for landing the big sharks in the industry. She had once talked her way into a $3.3 billion deal, which earned her a major promotion to Vice President of Strategic Partnerships.

Ava was well accomplished and utilized her talents to the best of her ability in all facets of life. Her greatest sacrifice of leaving Cal and her family to go to school gave her the ability to earn a Harvard degree on scholarship and propel her to the career of her dreams.

Yes, a red fitted skirt with a cream silk top would pair nicely with these leather high heels, Ava said to herself.

"I think you'd knock 'em dead wearing this silk number," Eric said in his rough, deep morning voice as he ever so gently caressed his fingertips down Ava's shoulder to her waist, kissing her neck.

Her heart pounded from his surprising presence, but she was quickly excited from his tender touch.

"Oh, you do," Ava said playfully. "But then all the focus would be on me rather than the client, and that won't seal the deal. Now will it?" she said with a coy smile as she turned around in his arms.

"Babe, you could close this deal in a brown paper sack. You have been prepping for months. I know you're going to knock this one out of the park."

Eric's confidence always filled Ava with the vigor to accept and overcome any challenge that was thrown her way. He reminded her of her dad in these moments.

"Well, if that's the case, then I guess I don't need to worry if my outfit matches." Ava laughed. Eric leaned in for a sweet but quick kiss. Ava thought the brisk kiss was unusual but had too much on her mind to press the issue.

As Ava spent the last few moments organizing her notes before heading to work, she prepared oatmeal for herself and asked Eric if he'd like anything to eat.

Ava's mother always said, making a hearty breakfast for her father was one of the greatest joys of her day, but Eric said he was heading to the gym and that he would grab something when he got back to his place.

With a kiss on the check, which reminded Ava of her dad's tender moments with her mother, Eric left her apartment.

Ava soaked in his kiss for a moment and anticipated their evening together after she came home from work. Eric often managed to surprise her in some way after she closed a key client.

Sometimes without even calling, he would have dinner ready with white long-stemmed roses waiting for her when she came home.

White roses were the first type of flower he had sent Ava at the office when he asked her out. Although Ava didn't even care for flowers, she thought it was endearing that he remembered the first flower he had given her.

The amount of confidence Eric had in Ava reaffirmed her feelings and made her fall more in love with him.

2

When Ava arrived at the doors of Truman Partners Inc., she smiled inwardly for working at such a prestigious firm so early in her career.

Being a recently promoted Vice President, Ava understood the power of her position but never forgot what it took to get there—long nights, relentless hours of work, and personal sacrifices she made along the way.

With perkiness to her morning step, she opened the massive glass doors and walked across the marble floor toward the elevators. The prestige of the building prepared Ava for the start of an amazing workday.

As the elevator doors opened on the thirtieth floor of the building, Ava stepped out and saw Silvia Beck, Truman's executive assistant. She was an older woman with gray strands that accented her dark hair and highlighted her olive skin.

Every morning, she greeted each person who stepped off the elevator with a kind smile and genuine curiosity for how their day was going. She made the mornings brighter at Truman Partners.

"Good Morning, Ms. Stillman. Planning for another exceptional day?" Silvia said with her bright smile.

"As a matter of fact, I am, Mrs. Beck," said Ava with upbeat happiness. "In fact, when Parker and Stokes arrive later this morning, please show them directly into the conference room. There's no need to wait today. I'm hoping our meeting won't take long."

"Certainly, Ms. Stillman," Silvia said in a more serious tone. "Can I get you any coffee from downstairs this morning? I'm headed there myself to grab a latte."

Since Ava was running on pure adrenaline in anticipation for her meeting, she regrettably declined. Typically, Ava enjoyed her coffee excursions in the morning, especially when she could share a ride on the elevator with Silvia.

As the Executive Assistant for nearly twenty years, she was able to shed light on many inner workings of the organization, including the latest rumors of what company would be acquired in the latest merger.

Truman Partners was a very successful firm that focused on mergers and acquisitions for their clients, along with a more recent adoption of acquiring smaller companies within the industry to ensure continual growth.

The CEO's motto, which was continuously stated in internal communications, was, "If you're not growing and moving forward, you might as well be backing up."

Approaching her corner office, Ava turned on the lights and took in the city skyline as she did every morning. The coffee table and surrounding gray leather sofas were lined with research she was working on earlier in the week.

Ava placed her briefcase and purse on the mahogany desk and took in a deep breath as she looked out the three large windows behind her desk. There were many days when Ava would look out her windows to escape the mundane office politics.

Ava settled into her chair and began checking e-mails. She saw one from her boss, Jackie Kullberg, who was considered a genius in her field and well-respected within the company for her business savvy. She was in her midforties and slender, with black hair that was always tightly pinned up, which mirrored her callous personality.

Although she had the respect of the higher-ups in the organization, due to her pristine legal sense and remarkable negotiation skills, which made millions for her clients and Truman Partners, she lacked the ability to connect with people.

Jackie had been promoted to Chief Operations Officer last April, which was a wonderful opportunity for her, but it also seemed to change how she managed Ava. Her personality was one of a Jekyll and Hyde effect.

Some days she was upbeat and a go-getter with a clear sense of direction for Ava. While other days, she piled hours of meaningless work for her to complete within an unrealistic time frame, knowing Ava would need to either work late nights or weekends to meet the deadline.

For the most part, Ava enjoyed working for Jackie. Her direct approach to managing allowed Ava the insight to know what needed to be accomplished with the flexibility of bringing in clients and closing deals with her own style, which enabled Ava to make a name for herself in the industry.

Jackie could be an inspiring mentor, but lately she lacked the motivation that once prevailed.

Ava read through Jackie's e-mail, which asked her to complete the due diligence reports before the end of the week for two clients the company was thinking of bringing on later in the year. Ava gave herself a nod of approval as she had completed this project earlier in the week.

She typed out an e-mail to Jackie, advising of her recommendations based upon her findings and a potential timeline for their request; however, she decided to send the e-mail after her meeting, so she could include the outcome with Parker and Stokes in her response.

Thinking of all the possible objections and how she would overcome them should they arise, Ava reviewed each page of the presentation.

Parker had been on board with the acquisition of the new company since the beginning, but Stokes needed more background and insurance that once the two companies came together, their assets would work together favorably to build growth rather than crumble due to the acquiring company's high overhead costs.

Ava took a moment to decompress before the meeting and looked out at the city below her. The white puffy clouds danced across the sky, while the sun peaked around the tall skyscrapers.

The peaceful scene reminded her that it would only be one month before she and Eric were lying on the beach in Jamaica, relaxing with a drink in their hands.

Depending on the outcome of the meeting, Ava hoped to leave early and surprise Eric at his apartment before he came home from work. Perhaps a home-cooked meal with rose petals leading into the bedroom would be a romantic way to say thank you, since he had been so supportive over the past few months with all the late nights and worked weekends.

The phone buzzed, as she was planning what to make Eric that night for dinner, informing her that Parker and Stokes were waiting in the conference room. Ava gathered her presentation, took a deep breath, and pushed away from her desk.

She put on her red blazer and smiled as she saw her reflection in the tall glass doors, thinking about what her mom always told her growing up. "Honey, there's just something about the right outfit before doing something important. It gives you a little courage and gumption. Now, go after your dream, sweetheart," she would say with a twinkle in her eye.

There was something about Momma's simple way of putting things that made so much sense, even in a highly important meeting in a New York conference room.

As Ava walked into the executive room, she found Parker and Stokes sitting together in the far right-hand corner of the room. They stood when Ava walked in the room. "Good morning, Ms. Stillman," they said, extending their hands for a firm shake.

Ava matched their resolve with a determined demeanor. "Good Morning, Mr. Parker, Mr. Stokes." She nodded. "Let's get started, shall we?" She extended her hand to take a seat.

Throughout the presentation, Ava highlighted the pros and cons of the potential acquisition as a recap. She explained that with the integration of the new company under the Parker, Stokes, and Associates umbrella, they would be able to hit the expansion goal they set for themselves.

The company they looked at obtaining had millions in assets, but they lacked the vision to turn their successful product into something that would continue to grow and evolve with technology.

Since Ava knew of Stokes's apprehension to the overhead, she prepared a section of the presentation to outline the trends and numbers should they combine the costs and eliminate the duplication, due to the merger.

Once Stokes saw this, his worries were eased, and he was impressed that Ava had taken the initiative and time to address his concerns while still providing a few solutions on how the company could continue to lower expenses once they merged.

After a quick two-hour meeting, Stokes and Parker signed the paperwork to move forward with the deal and shook Ava's hand in gratitude for all her remarkable talent and devotion to them.

"Ava, I know you must have several other clients, but we appreciate you always making us feel as though we are your number one priority. Being a family-oriented business, we take pride in our biggest assets, our people. So this deal was very important on multiple levels. It was more than the combining of assets. We needed to ensure our staff that they would still have a place to call home. Thank you for helping to make this deal a reality with your tactful research and arbitration," stated Parker.

"You are certainly welcome. I was elated to take your company on as a client. It's not every day when a million, excuse me, soon-to-be billion-dollar organization puts their team above the almighty dollar," Ava said, glowing with pride.

Stokes, relieved, said, "Thanks, Ava, for your competence on this. It has made an impression on us. One I am not likely to forget."

"I appreciate that, Mr. Stokes," Ava said. "I will compile the paperwork and begin processing the package. Once we have the signature from the other company, it will most likely take a few months for everything to be complete, but then you will officially be Parker, Stokes, Addison, and Associates.'"

Ava walked them to the elevator and wished them a good day. When the doors closed, she turned around and gave an immense smile to Silvia. "I assume congratulations are in order, Ms. Stillman?" Silvia said in a not-so-questioning manner.

"Yes, Mrs. Beck! It was a grand day on all accounts," Ava stated favorably.

"Excellent to hear," Silvia said enthusiastically.

Ava asked, "Silvia, can you please have a congratulatory basket sent to Parker, Stokes, and Associates, full of fruit, chocolates, and a bottle of Dom Pérignon with a note that says 'For all the successes you've had and for all the successes you've yet to accomplish, Parker, Stokes, Addison, and Associates, will achieve them together.'"

Staring in awe, Silvia said, "You never cease to amaze me, Ms. Stillman. The personal touch you afford to each and every client is impeccable. I've been in this industry for many years, and I have yet to see any executive care for their clients the way you do. It's a remarkable trait. One that I think others could take a cue from, if you ask me."

"Thank you, Mrs. Beck. I'm just doing my job. And who wouldn't want to receive a surprise basket with deliciously sweet treats for an amazing day of work," Ava said, smiling.

She walked back to her office and hammered out the package proposal that would be sent to Addison and Co. Luckily, Ava had previously spoken with Mark Addison when conducting her due diligence research, so she knew he was open to a merger, but it would need to be with the right match. "The perfect marriage," he said.

Before sending off the e-mail, Ava added, "Mark, I hope you're ready because I have an important question to ask you. What is Addison and Co. doing for the rest of its days?"

She hoped he would remember his reference to a potential merger when they had previously spoken; otherwise, the e-mail could be construed in a completely inappropriate way.

Noticing the time, Ava quickly sent off the e-mail to Mark and decided to head out to the grocery store to get the ingredients for her special dinner with Eric.

Ava thoroughly enjoyed cooking, a trait she learned from her mother. Although Ava wasn't the best cook, the love she put into her food and attention to detail always made her feel so accomplished after she finished preparing a meal.

Ava decided on chicken piccata with a side of homemade garlic mashed potatoes instead of linguine. For an appetizer, Ava thought bruschetta would pair nicely with a Pinot Noir. And for something sweet, she would pick up the dessert they got on their first date, a New York-style cheesecake topped with chocolate ganache.

What better way to plan for their future than to reminisce about their past.

3

Carrying the grocery bags into his apartment building, she saw Eric's neighbor Rose, an elderly woman who had a small white dog that she was taking outside.

"Hi, Rose. How are you doing today?" Ava said with a friendly smile.

"Oh, hello, dear. I'm getting along just fine. Mimi here has a cough though," Rose said, looking down at her dog.

"I'm sorry to hear that," Ava said, kneeling down to pet Mimi. "I hope you feel better soon, Mimi."

Rose saw the grocery bags and asked, "Are you preparing a nice meal for Eric this evening? You are such a sweetheart."

"I am. Hopefully, one that will remind him of our first date," Ava said with a beaming smile on her face. "Well, I better get going, Rose. I've got lots to prepare for this evening." They both said goodbye, and Ava headed to Eric's apartment.

Ava opened the door and headed to the kitchen to begin cooking her feast. She set the groceries down and suddenly heard a noise coming from the bedroom.

She didn't think Eric was home yet, so her heart began to race, thinking there was an intruder.

Looking around in a panic, she quickly grabbed a kitchen knife and her cell phone. She dialed Eric's number and slowly headed for the front door.

Ava's heart stopped for an instant when she heard the vibrating buzz of Eric's phone. As she turned her head and saw his phone sitting on the dining-room table, she knew he was home but didn't understand what he was doing home so early.

Her mind raced and immediately went to the worst-case scenario—he was with another woman. Ava scratched that thought from her mind. Eric loved her, and they were going to get married; he wouldn't do that to her.

Ava placed the knife back in the kitchen and slowly walked toward the bedroom. As she tiptoed to the door, she heard a woman's voice, and Ava froze as if time stood still. Her heart pounded, and in disbelief, her head began to spin in a million different directions.

She was frozen and couldn't move another step. Her heart was pounding so loud; she could hear the blood coursing through her veins.

Ava thought Eric could surely hear her outside his bed-room door. Realizing Eric was with another woman crippled Ava so much that she sank to the ground.

"How could this be happening? I thought he loved me," Ava whispered to herself, feeling defeated. Her head hung low as her hair fell over her face.

Ava's eyes began to fill with water, but before the first drop hit the floor, a raging sense of anger festered inside.

As if a light had ignited inside her, Ava slowly rolled her head up, turned her eyes up toward the door handle, and realized everything they had built together was shattered.

Only seeing red from the hurt and anger roaring deep inside her, she picked herself up off the floor, grabbed the door, and flung it open.

Releasing the noise inside her head, she heard herself screaming a shrewd sound that she didn't know existed. Roaring at the top of her lungs with such distain, Ava shouted, "Eric! What the hell are you doing?"

Looking around for something to throw at him, her body halted at the sight that lay before her eyes. Eric was entangled in his sheets with not only any woman but with Jackie.

"Are you fucking kidding me?" Ava said as she spat the words out of her mouth, so hurt and angry.

Ava thought she would be physically ill from seeing them together. Eric was shocked that Ava was not at work, "Ava! What are you doing here?"

"What am I doing here? That's what you have to say to me? What am I doing here? You son of a bitch," Ava said.

Jackie looked at me with a coy smile and said, "Ava, I thought you'd be working on the newest assignment I had given you."

It was in that moment that Ava began putting it all together. All those endless nights and weekends full of meaningless work was truly worthless and a waste of time. She had only over-loaded her plate so she could shack up with Eric.

Ava's blood began to boil. She ran to the bed and yanked the sheets with such force she knocked Jackie on the floor inadvertently, but she wasn't upset with the outcome.

"You shut your mouth, home-wrecker. I'll get to you in a minute," Ava said as her eyes narrowed in on her and deciding on the ramifications of hitting her.

Eric approached her, trying to calm Ava down and apologizing profusely that she had found out. Screaming to remove his hands from her, Ava slapped him across the face so hard her hand burned with the sting of satisfaction.

Eric grabbed his face in disbelief and slowly stepped backward from Ava, realizing that he had hurt her to an extent that he could not fix with an apology.

Jackie picked herself up off the floor and wrapped her body in the satin sheets. With her typical high-powering demeanor, she sauntered over to where Ava stood.

"Don't take one more step toward me, you repulsive, demented bitch," Ava spouted with such hatred.

"Oh, my sweet Ava. Did you really think that Eric would be faithful to you?" Jackie pushed on with her defeating words as she stared deep into Ava's eyes, watching the reluctant tears fall.

"What about this man says loyal? You two would never have worked out."

Taking in the words that Jackie was saying, knowing that this situation would not only change Ava's personal relationship but her professional one as well, Ava said, "Jackie, you have always been callous, but I didn't realize you were deliberately destructive. And Eric. Really? You could sleep with anyone you wanted, yet you go after my boyfriend. You're pathetic."

"Oh, I wasn't the one who pursued him, Ava. I just simply didn't say no."

Ava looked at Eric in disbelief as he stood in the corner of the room, observing the whole conversation as though an innocent bystander.

Eric closed his eyes and lowered his head as if to admit his last secret had been exposed after Jackie's comment.

"I was doing you a favor," Jackie said.

"Yes. I suppose you were. In fact, I would say you two deserve each other, Jackie."

Looking at Eric, Ava uttered in an eerily calm, deep voice, "You're a selfish son of a bitch who deserves to rot in hell. And you"—turning her attention to Jackie—"you're a heartless woman who will never find love, just someone desperate to screw anything that walks."

Ava whipped around and walked out of the room with her head held high.

She grabbed her purse off the counter and stormed out of Eric's apartment, slamming the door.

4

Ava made it to the corner before she let out a single breath, which quickly turned into a river of tears. She was a mess of emotions—angry, sad, hurt, and ashamed.

As if Mother Nature knew her state of mind, the darkened storm clouds rolled above, and the skies opened up with heavy raindrops.

How appropriate, Ava thought. She looked up through her tear-soaked eyes and spotted a bar that she and her friends would often go.

Making her way through the flooding rain and crazy New York traffic, she opened the bar's door to find a relatively noisy atmosphere.

"Perfect! Noise to fill my head so I don't have to think," Ava muttered. She was ultimately relieved that it was raining outside as her runny mascara and watered-down face blended in with the looming weather.

She found a vacant seat at the corner of the bar that was out of the main stream of traffic. Ava took off her soaked jacket and hung it on the back of her chair. As she turned around, she saw a small stage where she had sung karaoke one night with her friends.

Reliving the memory, she pictured all of them taking shots at the bar to muster up the courage to sing the ultimate girl song, "Girls Just Want to Have Fun." The reminiscing daydream of such an exciting evening was short-lived when she snapped back to reality thinking, *If she was out with her friends, what would Eric have been doing?*

Ava began reliving every memory she had over the past year, wondering if every time they weren't together, had Eric been cheating on her. *How many women were there? Was it just Jackie? As if that wasn't bad enough.*

She felt as though the last year with Eric was a web of lies and deceit. Trying to decipher truth from what was once her reality was a task Ava thought she would never have to face.

How could someone lie to another this way? Especially someone they loved. It didn't seem right or fair.

Getting lost in her own mind, Ava didn't hear or see the bartender in front of her. "Excuse me, Ms. Are you okay? Would you like something to drink?"

"Oh, I'm sorry. I guess I was somewhere else," Ava stated lowly.

"Yeah, I could tell," he said.

Ava thought of going off on the guy, but instead she gave up and felt defeated. "Yes, a long island please. And keep 'em coming."

He smiled as though he was smirking, but something about Ava's disposition must have said, "I'm not in the mood for any shenanigans." So he politely said, "Sure thing."

Ava began sipping away her sorrows and thinking about what her next move would be both personally and professionally.

Now that her boss had been screwing her boyfriend, she couldn't exactly go back to work for the same dreadful woman. *Hell no! Absolutely not.*

Ava thought to herself, *Maybe I could start my own business with the client base that I had built up over the years.* Her inner voice came shining through to say, *No, of course you can't do that. You'll be seen as too young and inexperienced to be the CEO of a company.* But Ava knew full well that without her skills, Truman Partners wouldn't have sealed the deal with some of the more prestigious clients on their books. *If I couldn't break away from the company, perhaps I could persuade human resources to fire Jackie for her efforts to keep me working on frivolous projects just so she could screw my boyfriend. There had to be some clause about that in the HR handbook. Rule 1: No stealing from the company. Rule 2: No sexual harassment. Rule 3: No screwing your employee's significant other.*

As if her day couldn't get any worse, a gentleman who had clearly been at the bar since it opened sauntered over and sat beside her, hoping for a tantalizing conversation followed by a night of pleasure.

Ava looked up from her glass to find the white imprint of where he wore his wedding ring, and she lost her composure.

"Are you kidding me!" Ava yelled a little louder than what she had intended. The man, who was rambling on about what he did and how much money he made, stopped midsentence.

"You came over here to what? Get a date? A one-night stand? What?" Ava only saw red. She didn't even let the man speak to defend himself.

"You may be drunk, but that is no excuse to cheat on your wife. You think just because you take off your ring, that women don't see the white circle around your finger where your wedding ring should be? You should feel ashamed of yourself. Your wife, whoever she is, doesn't deserve a lousy, pathetic excuse of a husband like you. What is wrong with you?" Ava retorted.

The man, without saying a word, picked up his drink, lifted himself up off his chair, and nodded to Ava in an apologetic manner. He quickly finished his drink, paid the barkeep, and left.

Ava finished her first drink and motioned to the bartender for another when her phone rang. She meant to turn it off when she got inside the bar but must have forgotten.

Looking down at the screen, she saw it was a number she didn't recognize. *It can go to voice mail,* she thought.

The number rang two more times before Ava finally answered the call. "Yes, how can I help you?" she said abruptly.

"Pardon me. Is this Ava, Ava Stillman?" The voice on the other end sounded ominous. Ava's heart sank when she realized it was an Iowa area code.

"Yes, this is she," Ava responded with a nervous tone. "Ms. Stillman, this is Dr. Sophie with the Meadow Brook Hospital in Keokuk, Iowa. We have your mother, Shelby Stillman, here, and she is in critical condition. Are you able to come here immediately?"

"Of course, I will be there as soon as I can. Is she okay? What happened?" Ava answered in a panic.

Dr. Sophie responded in a calming voice, "Ms. Stillman, I'd prefer to talk in person once you arrive. Your mother is stable for now, but we think it's best if you can get here as soon as possible."

The call ended, and Ava was visibly distraught. Her world was flipped upside down, and now her mother was in the hospital in a stable condition caused by something serious enough the doctors needed next of kin there immediately. Knowing she had to leave instantly, she flagged down the bartender.

Before she could ask for the check, he handed her the bill with a handwritten note that said, "This one is on me. Hope your day gets a little brighter."

Ava mustered up enough energy to give a kind smile and decided to keep the note for hope that decent men do exist.

Making her way back to her apartment, Ava quickly packed a bag. She booked the earliest flight that would leave New York and sent an e-mail to HR, cc'ing Jackie, stating that there had been a family emergency, and she would be out the following week.

At this point, Ava didn't care how this made her look in Jackie's eyes. She just knew that her mother needed her, and she was heading home because in that moment, nothing else mattered.

5

The flight seemed to take forever to land. Ava was so anxious; she could hardly sit still. To pass the time, she decided to get out her laptop and work on the plane.

Scrolling through e-mails, she saw a response from HR.

Ava,

We are so sorry to hear of your emergency. Our thoughts and prayers go out to you and your family. We hope for a speedy recovery.

Jackie is out of the office right now, but you have the time accrued. Please take the time you need, and keep us updated. Let us know if there's anything that we can do for you on behalf of Truman Partners.

Carol-Ann Peters
EVP of Human Resources

Truman Partners

"I bet she's out of the office," Ava mumbled under her breath.

She proceeded to read her e-mails when she saw a response from Mark. Hurrying to see his reply, she opened the e-mail to see in bold text, "My answer, Ms. Stillman, is yes!"

Even in Ava's unimaginable state, she was beginning to see at least one ray of sunshine in her otherwise dismal day.

Ava continued to read Mark's e-mail with a faint but recognizable smile on her face.

Ava,

Thank you for your e-mail. To put it simply, my answer, Ms. Stillman, is yes!

The proposal you presented was nothing short of agreeable and favorable to both parties—the best kind of partnership, if you ask me.

Section 3.1 may need some tweaking as I'd like to see a succession plan built in that provides career opportunities for my people as well.

This company wouldn't have grown as it did without my people, and I don't want them thinking that their jobs are in jeopardy because of this merger.

Additionally, I agree with the name proposal as well as Parker and Stokes's amendment regarding the efficiency factor to help elevate the newly merged company to grow quicker so our revenue can reach the previously discussed goals.

Ava, it has been a pleasure working with you on this endeavor. Your passion for creating win-win relationships is uncanny. The drive and tenacity you exude will certainly take you far in your career.

I would certainly be a favorable reference should you ever need one in the future, but before you look elsewhere, please do me the favor and keep Parker, Stokes, Addison, and Associates in mind.

Talent such as yours is a rare gem that deserves to shine, and we would be happy to help make that happen.

Sincerely,
Mark Addison
CEO/President
Addison and Co.

Ava was astounded at his appreciative words and elated that Mark decided to move forward with the merger.

Personally, Ava thought the coming together of these two organizations was an excellent partnership for all involved participants from the bottom up to the executive level.

Ava sent off a response to Mark, thanking him for his feedback and letting him know that she would address his changes once she returned to the office from her family emergency.

Soon after she sent the e-mail, the pilot came over the intercom and said they were making their final descent to the airport.

* * *

Rushing through the hospital doors, Ava immediately made eye contact with the nurse at the duty station. "My mom was brought here. Shelby Stillman. Dr. Sophie called and asked me to come immediately."

"And your name, dear?" the nurse said in response.

"Oh, sorry. Ava Stillman. Is she okay? Where is she?" Ava said in a panic.

"I'm sorry. I am not at liberty to disclose any patient information, but I will page Dr. Sophie. She will speak with you. Please have a seat and wait for her," the nurse said with kind words as she pointed to the waiting area.

Ava waited for what seemed like hours for the doctor to arrive. "Ms. Stillman?" Dr. Sophie said, reading a chart and looking around for who answered her call.

"I'm here. How's my mother? No one has told me anything, and I'm going to lose whatever sanity I have left. Please tell me something." Ava managed to stumble out.

"Ms. Stillman, thank you for coming. Please follow me, and I will take you to your mother," Dr. Sophie said, ushering her to a long, narrow hallway. "We believe your mother experienced a minor stroke and slipped into a coma."

Ava gasped at the idea that her mom might not be coming home. First it was her dad three years ago, and now her mom. She didn't know how this day could possibly get any worse.

She couldn't imagine her world without her mother, knowing one day that yes, she would pass on, but not now. Not today.

"We're not sure when or if she will wake up, but we are hopeful. Her vital signs are strong, and she is responding well to the medication."

"Then why hasn't she woken up yet?" Ava asked inquisitively.

"Well, sometimes, the body needs more time to recover and heal itself from certain damages or traumas that have occurred. It is my understanding that the neighbor found her this morning. Let's give it some time and reevaluate tomorrow morning."

Dr. Sophie sounded so confident that her mom would wake up that it gave Ava hope.

Ava slowly walked toward her mom who was lying helplessly in the bed. Taking in the impersonal white room with the consistent beeping of the machines, Ava drifted back to three years ago when she was in the very same hospital watching her father pass away.

Those days were so dark and bleak. Ava didn't know how she would get past them, but she somehow did. Ava threw herself into her work with countless hours of research and took on more clients than some associates did in a year. She had propelled her career to unknown heights within the company.

Then she met Eric, and things finally started to fall into place, or so she thought. The moment she began to think of Eric and all their wonderful memories, a wave of emotions rolled over her.

How could he have done this to her? To them? It didn't make any sense. She thought they were happy together. She thought he was going to propose for goodness' sake.

"How stupid was I to think he was going to propose?" Ava said out loud, not realizing a nurse just walked in the room.

"Who is proposing?" the nurse said blissfully as she came in to check her mom's fluids.

Squirming and feeling uncomfortable, Ava said, "Oh, no one. Just a friend of mine back home."

"Weddings are always great—the coming together of two people so in love. It just makes you realize how wonderful this life can really be. Don't you think?" the nurse said as she was clearly thinking of her own wedding day.

Not wanting to burst her bubble that some relationships weren't fairy tales, Ava politely responded, "Certainly. Anything is possible." Changing topics, Ava asked, "How's she doing?"

"Oh, she's a fighter for sure," she said proudly as if she knew her. Ava glanced at her nametag—Gracie.

The name rang a bell from conversations she had with her mom, but she couldn't quite place the relationship.

"Mrs. Stillman is hanging in there. She volunteers here a few days a week, always bubbly and telling fascinating stories." Gracie hesitated as she turned to Ava and asked, "Are you Ava, her daughter?"

Ava nodded. "Wow, I feel like I know you," said Gracie. "I'm sure this is odd, me talking to you as if I know you, but your mother was always talking about her top executive daughter doing amazing things in New York City. She said you were changing the world," Gracie said, trailing off as if in a state of awe.

Snickering a bit, Ava said, "I don't know about changing the world. I simply help companies find each other who could do more good together than apart."

"Sounds like saving the world to those companies whose lives you change." Gracie paused for a minute and blurted out, "You're like a professional matchmaker for big companies!"

Ava hadn't thought about it like that before, but she laughed and said, "I guess in a way, I am." Her eyes glimmered with a smile momentarily until she came back to reality, realizing where she was.

"Gracie, what about my mom? Can you tell me anything?" Ava asked in desperation.

"Honestly, Ava, your mom didn't show any of the early warning signs of a stroke. No weakness in her arm or difficulty speaking while here at the hospital. Did you notice any difference last time you spoke with her?"

"No, nothing seemed out of the ordinary," Ava said distantly as she tried to remember the last time they spoke.

They discussed her coming home for Thanksgiving in a few months, and Ava mentioned that she would try to get away from work but that she might be closing a big merger for one of her clients.

Thinking back on their phone call, Ava wished she had said that she would be home for the holidays without hesitation. Nothing came before family in Ava's mind.

"Ava, I'm not allowed to disclose patient information as I'm not a primary physician overseeing your mom, but I can inform you of the different types of stroke if you are not familiar with them so you can have background information."

"Your mom always said you loved your research and yearned for as much understanding before you went in to see a client. She said it helped you feel mentally prepared for any outcome."

Ava smiled gently. "Yes, she is correct. Please tell me, Gracie."

Gracie sat Ava down in the chair next to Shelby's bed and began describing the three types of stroke.

"A stroke happens when blood flow to part of the brain is interrupted. Ischemic is more common and can be induced by atherosclerosis, irregular heartbeat, heart attack, or injury to blood vessels. Does that make sense?" Gracie said as to make sure Ava understood.

Ava nodded, absorbing it all, and Gracie continued, "The second, Hemorrhagic, starts suddenly and are often more severe with intense headaches, confusion, nausea, or passing out."

"Finally, Transient Ischemic Attacks is a temporary blockage in blood flow to the brain, often referred to as a ministroke, which is a warning sign for the first type I mentioned."

Before continuing, Gracie asked if Ava was okay and if she should continue. Ava nodded again even though she was plainly overwhelmed with the information.

"Since strokes cause damage to brain cells, complications can arise, such as seizures, cognitive problems, fluid buildup, swelling, and bleeding into the brain, dizziness, sudden numbness, or heart failure if left untreated or not seen by a doctor immediately."

Grabbing Ava's hand, Gracie smiled sweetly and said, "But don't you worry, Ava. Your mom was in good hands when she arrived here at Meadow Brook, and now that you're here, I'm sure that she will be awake in no time."

The stress of the day had weighed heavily on Ava. She nodded and asked Gracie if she could have some time alone with her mom. Gracie understood her need to talk to her mom and kindly left the room.

Ava peered out the window and remembered just how peaceful the night sky could be without the distraction of city lights. Looking back at her mom, Ava's eyes started to well up with tears.

"Mom, you have to wake up. I need you now more than you know. Your words of wisdom lift me up and make me think I can conquer the world. I wish you would have said something if you weren't feeling well. I would have come back, Mom. I would have," Ava said, getting choked up and barely able to talk.

Ava once read that speaking to people in comas could be therapeutic for both parties and helpful for the patient's recovery. She felt guilty for not being there for her mom when she had the stroke.

She stumbled as she told her mom what happened with Eric and began crying uncontrollably.

Not having her mother to respond or offer guidance left Ava empty inside. All she wanted was for her mom to wake up and tell her everything was going to be okay. After only losing her dad three years earlier, Ava didn't know how to cope if she lost her mom.

"Mom." Ava sobbed. "Just wake up. Please. I need you. I'm not ready to say goodbye yet. Please, Mom."

Night had passed, and dawn crept through the window. Breaking through the large oak trees, the sunlight danced on the blankets and across Ava's face as she began to wake. She had fallen asleep from her emotionally exhausting conversation with her mom last night.

Looking at her mom and hearing the same constant beeps, Ava felt some sense of comfort that things hadn't taken a turn for the worst last night. She got up from the bedside and made her way to the bathroom to freshen up and brush her teeth.

As Ava caught a glance of herself in the mirror, she hardly recognized the woman standing before her, so visibly spent and drained from all the goodness that life had to offer. She began doubting her own strength and thinking of excuses for Eric.

"Maybe I did work too much or too long of hours for a healthy relationship," Ava said to herself. But then a voice inside her head said, *Snap out of it. He did this to you, not the other way around. This is his fault. He cheated. He was unfaithful, not you.*

And with that, Ava spit out her toothpaste with a refreshing taste in her mouth and a renewed sense of recognition for her own self-worth.

"I am worth loving," Ava stated to herself in the mirror. "And don't you forget it," she said with a nod of approval and a turn of enthusiasm toward the door.

Ava, busily rummaging through her purse for ChapStick, told her mom that she was headed downstairs for a warm cup of coffee and that she would be back in a few minutes.

As she walked toward the door, Ava heard, "Okay, dear. I'll see you when you get back."

Running to the bedside, Ava burst into tears and screamed, "Mom, Mom, you're awake! Nurse, Gracie, someone, please help. My mom's awake."

Shelby didn't understand what all the fuss was about. "Honey, are you feeling okay? You don't look very well. You look tired and sad," Shelby said matter-of-factly.

"Mom, you've been in a coma," Ava stammered.

"What? I don't understand. Wait, where am I?" Shelby said as she looked around the hospital room.

"Am I at Meadow Brook? It's not my volunteer day, is it? What are you doing here instead of New York?" Shelby asked, perplexed.

Just as Ava was about to answer her mom's questions, Dr. Sophie, Gracie, and a few other attendees rushed into the room. "Mrs. Stillman, my name is Dr. Sophie. Do you know where you are?" Dr. Sophie asked directly.

Clearing her throat to take in the severity of the situation, Shelby responded, "Yes, I know where I am. Meadow Brook Hospital. I volunteer here a few days a week. I know exactly who you are Dr. Sophie. Why am I lying in this bed?"

"We believe you suffered a stroke yesterday. Your neighbor found you and called the ambulance. They rushed you here to my care. Can you tell me the last thing you remember?"

Shelby looked around, and getting confused, answered, "I remember getting ready to go for a walk with Barbara. I walked out to the kitchen and grabbed a glass of water. I felt light-headed, so I sat down for a minute. That is the last thing I remember."

"Mrs. Stillman, you are a very lucky woman. Because you sat down, you didn't fall and hurt yourself with a contusion or worse. And Barbara might have saved your life. She must have just missed you passing out when she arrived for your walk," Dr. Sophie said in a relaxed yet firm manner.

"We're going to continue to monitor you for the next forty-eight hours, and then we will need to release you into someone's care. Is there someone who can take care of you for the next week or so?" Dr. Sophie asked.

Before Shelby was able to answer, Ava interjected, "Yes, I will be here, and I can take care of her." The look exchanged between Ava and her mother was unmistakable. The bond they had always had only grew stronger after her father had passed.

Ava felt empowered now that her mother was awake. Shelby needed Ava's help to get better, and Ava was prepared to do anything to help her mother recover.

"Okay, then it's settled," Dr. Sophie said. "If your vitals remain stable for the next forty-eight hours, then we will release you into your daughter's care. However, I want you to have a follow-up with your primary in one week from your discharge date. This will allow enough time to elapse so we can monitor you and see if there is any damage associated with the stroke."

"Yes, Doctor," Shelby said eagerly.

However, Dr. Sophie wasn't finished instructing her mother on the potential dangers for stroke victims. "I am also putting you on blood pressure medication."

Turning toward Ava, she continued, "I will provide enough meds for a few days, but you will need to get this script filled at your mother's local pharmacy." Dr. Sophie looked back toward Shelby. "Mrs. Stillman, it is very important that you take the medication. This will help your body remove any undue pressure being put on your body. Shelby, you sustained a minor stroke, but it does not appear that you are experiencing any of the major complications we look for, such as paralysis, loss of muscle control, difficulty speaking, or memory loss. If you begin to experience any of these symptoms or you feel dizzy again, you need to come straight to the hospital. Do you understand what I am saying?"

Looking at Shelby firmly, Dr. Sophie wanted to ensure she understood the severity of her condition. Even though she wasn't experiencing any pain at the moment, that did not mean they were out of the woods just yet.

Ava soaked in all the information and took mental notes. Shelby, who often found the positives in any situation, seemed pleasantly relaxed by the doctor's barking orders.

"Yes, Dr. Sophie, I understand exactly what you're saying. If I don't take the medicine, I could end up not waking up one day, but I am awake now and feeling better than ever," Shelby said with a smile only a mother could give that embraced you completely while being on the other side of the room.

"Okay, Mom, let's focus on the next forty-eight hours and get you home," Ava said with a forced smile.

6

The next two days were long but less stressful since Shelby was awake. Ava never left her bedside, day or night. "You need to sleep, honey. Why don't you go home and sleep in your old bed."

"Mom, I'm not going anywhere until you are able to leave this hospital," Ava said in a respectful tone.

"Well, then, what should we do? Play a game of cards, talk about work or Eric, or maybe go for a walk?" Shelby said, upbeat as always.

With all the recent events, Ava forgot that her mom wasn't awake to hear her story of Eric. So with a heavy heart, Ava recounted what she walked in on the other day with Eric and Jackie. Although there were fewer tears with this round, the emotions were high and the images were still fresh in her mind.

"Oh, sweetheart, I am so sorry that you had to go through that awful mess. I wish I could take your pain away and make it better," Shelby said as she stroked her daughter's hair.

"It's his loss. You deserve someone who is going to love you, respect you, and treat you like the wonderful woman you are. Never forget how strong you really are, honey."

"Mom, I think you have to say that. It's in the Mother's Handbook or something," Ava said laughingly.

"Oh no, I don't have to say anything just because I'm your mother. God blessed me with one special child that I had the pleasure of watching grow up, learn new things, discover her amazing abilities, and see the strong, independent woman she has become. You see, Ava, it's my duty as your mom to help you see everything that you can't see," Shelby said, lifting Ava's face to hers.

As Shelby kissed her daughter's forehead, she whispered, "Never forget how truly special you are and how much you are loved, especially by me."

With that, Ava's heart felt warm and full of love—a feeling she had been missing for a long time but didn't realize until that moment.

The day had finally come for Ava to take her mom home. Dr. Sophie discharged her from the hospital with the notion that she would be relaxing, taking it easy, and following up with her primary physician in the coming days.

As Ava wheeled Shelby outside, the birds were chirping, the breeze blew through the trees as if they swayed to the beat of the bird's song, and the sun beamed down on them through the fluffy white clouds. They both took a deep breath and paused to enjoy the beautiful outdoors together.

Getting into the passenger side of the car, Shelby saw a flashback from when Ava was fifteen and just learning how to drive. John, Ava's father, was incredibly patient with her as she took the wheel.

He would always say, "Honey, a car is a weapon. Respect it and the road. Know your surroundings. Be aware of others because they may not be aware of you. Always be careful when you get behind the wheel of a car because I need to have you home in one piece."

Ava would blush after John would say the last part, but Shelby thought it would stick with her as it made a fond impression. He always qualified it with "understand," as if Ava wasn't paying attention.

Looking at Ava drive down Main Street, Shelby was brought back to the present. "Ava, how long are you able to stay before you have to go back to New York?"

"I told you, Mom, I'm going to stay as long as I need to so I can take care of you."

"Well, what does work say? How do you think you will handle your situation with Jackie at work?" Shelby was typically direct in her questioning, so it only reminded Ava that she was feeling better.

Smiling inside that her mom was back to herself, Ava responded, "I'm not sure what work will say. I'm certain I can work remotely for a few weeks. And as far as Jackie goes, I don't know. I guess I'll find another department to work for or maybe ask for a new supervisor. Or who knows, maybe I'll go off and start my own company."

They both laughed, and then Shelby said in all seriousness, "You know, Ava, you can do anything you put your mind to. So if you wanted to start up your own company, you could."

Laughing off the idea, Ava said, "Ha, yeah, I don't think I'd have the capital one would need to start merging million—no, I'm sorry—billion-dollar companies. But thanks for the vote of confidence, Mom."

"Well, honey, whether you know it or not, you have the ability to do anything to set your mind to. You may not see how strong you are, but I do. And so does Jackie for that matter. Why do you think she messed around with Eric?"

"I know you say she's a tiger in the industry, but what kind of person is so insecure with themselves that they knowingly cheat with someone that they know is with someone else and that they are around on a daily basis. A callous, heartless person who doesn't love themselves, that's who."

Ava took in what her mom said, even though she really didn't want to hear anything more about Eric or Jackie. But in all the chaos and anger, she had not given much thought as to why Jackie knowingly had an affair with Eric.

Putting the thought behind her, Ava pulled into the driveway and saw her childhood home. It had been a few years since she had been home, but every memory came rushing back to her.

Ava flew back on the anniversary of her father's death so her mom wouldn't have to visit her dad's grave alone. The following anniversary, Shelby met Ava in New York City for a girls' weekend getaway. The time she spent with her mother was always so precious to her.

Shelby began getting out of the car when Ava saw her and yelled without realizing, "Mom, wait for me! I can help you."

"I don't need help getting out of the damn car. I'm not crippled, you know. At least not yet," Shelby said with a snappy retort.

"Mom, you know that's not what I meant, and don't say that. I know you're not crippled. I just wanted to help you out of the car and into the house. You've had a stroke for crying out loud," Ava said.

Ava made her way around the car in time for Shelby to have just shut the door. They exchanged a familiar look of playful disagreement and continued in the house.

Searching for the familiar smell of home, Ava opened the front door. Sweet cream, lavender, and hibiscus swept through Ava's memories like a floodgate.

Every time she opened her door in New York, she would imagine it smelled like her parents' house.

"Home sweet home," Shelby said with a gentle sigh. Even though it had been three years, they both still lingered at the door, waiting to hear John's voice or smell his cologne in the air.

"Yes, finally." Ava sounded exhausted.

"Mom, would you like something to eat or drink? I'll make you anything you want."

Shelby smiled at Ava. "Ah, thanks, but I really just want to go relax out back and soak in the rest of this beautiful day. Will you join me?"

With chipper excitement, Ava placed her bags next to the table in the foyer. "Of course. I'll grab something to drink for us, and we can head out there."

Ava went to the kitchen where she had helped her mom prepare many dinners and desserts throughout her youth. She loved cooking and baking with her mom.

They would talk dreams, boys, careers—anything and everything. Her dad would always come in the kitchen trying to pick at whatever it was that they were making. Ava thought she got that quirk from him because she would always find herself tasting food as she cooked.

Opening the cabinet door, Ava grabbed two glasses and filled them with the pitcher of cold lemonade that seemed to live in the refrigerator but was always full. This was one of John's habits that Shelby couldn't break after forty years of marriage.

Shelby and Ava walked out to the back patio and sat in the two Adirondack chairs that overlooked a large pond with rolling hills and mountains.

The sight was breathtaking and brought back many fond memories for Ava when she was growing up.

The chairs were placed strategically in front of a large in-ground firepit that John built with his own two hands. Ava always admired her dad for being so handy.

"You can always fix something that's broken, Ava. Remember that," he would say.

Ava often reminisced over things her dad had said. It helped her remember him as if he were still there with her. She envisioned her future husband to have a similar passion for fixing things for his family.

"So, my dear, what's it going to be?" Shelby said, watching Ava with a look of determination to solve the world's problems right then and there.

"With what, Mom? Work?" Ava said, weary. Shelby shook her head and then looked out at the view, almost like she was searching for her daughter's answer.

"I'm not sure what to do. I would love to keep doing what I'm doing and not have to work with Jackie or see Eric ever again, but I'm not sure that is realistic."

Shelby paused a minute before answering, "Well, if that's what you want to do, but don't think it's possible, then what can you do to make sure you continue doing what you love?"

Ava chuckled a little to herself, "Mom, you are quite the insightful person today, aren't you?" They both smiled and laughed.

"Well, honey, there's no sense in doing something with the majority of your day if you are miserable because of who is around you. You need to muster up the courage to do what needs to be done, whatever that is, and find your happy place."

"Happy place. That's what Dad would always say. I miss him, Mom. So much, it hurts. Sometimes, I swear he is still here. But I know that's silly," Ava said sorrowfully.

"I know what you mean. I have conversations with him all the time," Shelby said, trailing off.

Ava remembered what Dr. Sophie had said about memory and understating complications that stroke victims can experience.

Shelby sensed Ava's worry. "Not that he answers back. I know he's not really there, Ava, but it gets lonely in this house all by myself sometimes. So I pretend as though he's in the other room, and I talk to him. You probably don't understand, sweetheart, and I hope you never have to."

Ava patted her mom's hand, and they sat quietly, taking in the view.

7

A little later, Shelby took a nap, and Ava decided to unpack and catch up on work. Opening the door to her childhood bedroom, she felt time stand still.

Pictures of high school friends still remained in her dresser mirror. Her academic and athletic trophies, which were treasured items at the time, collected dust on the bookshelf next to the bed.

Finally, her eyes made their way over to the nightstand, where she saw the last picture of her and Cal at the summer carnival after graduation.

Ava dropped her bags on the bed and took the picture frame in her hand. He meant everything to Ava in high school. If she were being honest with herself, he still held a special place in her heart.

There was something about a first true love that never faded—no matter what might happen in a person's life.

With a heavy heart, she placed the picture frame down and sighed heavily as she thought about where he was now—most likely with a perfect family and gorgeous wife.

Without much thought, Ava rummaged through her purse to find her phone, which had been turned off since she arrived at the hospital a few days ago.

Wanting to get a head start on some work, she began listening to voice mails while setting up her laptop.

Hearing Eric's voice sent sharp, needlelike pings through Ava's chest, forcing her to freeze. Her heart pounded with every word he spoke. She felt her blood pulsate in her ears down to her toes.

His voice sounded sincere, but Ava wasn't going to be fooled again. The more she thought of everything he had done and how he deceived her for so long, the more disgusted she became.

The lies and deceitfulness were enough to make any woman come unglued. Ava wondered why he was trying to smooth things over and what he really wanted by calling.

She found her way to the white wicker chair at her desk and sank into the seat. After listening to what seemed like a hundred messages of Eric apologizing and pleading that it would never happen again, Ava's emotions were spinning.

How could I have been so stupid not to have seen anything that was going on? Ava thought to herself.

She replayed everything in her mind from the beginning of their relationship, wondering how she missed all the signs.

She thought about every time he worked late or canceled dates last minute. Was everything a lie? Did he love her at all, or was everything they had together a facade that he used as a fail-safe if things didn't work out with Jackie?

Ava wondered if she was his second choice, Eric's backup plan, or was it once love that went wrong because of her long nights pursuing a career that no man would come between.

But he was cheating and with Jackie no less. Feeling so defeated and worn down, Ava sank deeper into her chair, trying to decipher between reality and lies. How would she face everyone at work and their friends?

Ava thought Eric was proposing soon. "What a fool I was," she said, disheartened.

Pushing the idea of Eric aside, Ava put her phone on silent and began working from her childhood room.

Sifting through hundreds of e-mails, Ava followed up initially with Parker, Stokes, and Addison regarding their upcoming merger.

She wanted to fill them in on the additional amendments that would be included in the final contracts as well as letting them know that she would be working remotely for the next few weeks as her mother recovered from a stroke.

After updating their paperwork on the upcoming merger, Ava would typically send them to Jackie for review. With the recent events, Ava did not want to continue working for Jackie no matter how beneficial it was to her career.

Thinking logistically about her predicament, Ava decided to send the final paperwork to the president of the company and copy Jackie, since these prestigious clients would make an impact on the bottom line and reputation.

Although this might raise a few red flags with upper management, Ava intended to keep her head held high and maintain her professional composure.

Ava was loyal to her clients and could not leave them exposed by simply resigning. She had planned to complete this last merger among Parker, Stokes, and Addison, and then find another job.

Perhaps, she would return one of the ten headhunter's calls that continually reached out to her.

As Ava began to think of options that might exist for her, a shimmer of hope began to appear. Ava could see a life that didn't include Eric or Jackie. Nevertheless, that future seemed too far away but present, nonetheless.

Looking around the room for a distraction, Ava saw pictures of her and Cal throughout their senior year of high school. A genuine smile graced her face as she reminisced over their memories together.

Ava wondered how it was possible to still remember the way he smelled or his tenderness. Cal was so sweet, respectful, and understanding.

He knew the way to her heart. *But we were so young,* thought Ava. *Could it really have been lifelong love and not just a teenage romance?*

She questioned her feelings for him when they were younger. *Was it love? Could it have worked?* Ava put a conscious effort into not giving into the what if questions, but she was brought back to what made her leave Cal.

Ava thought about the sleepless nights she faced in this very room as she debated on going to school in Massachusetts or staying with the love of her life.

The choice was difficult, but as Ava weighed the options and took into consideration her scholarship, she decided leaving was the best thing for her future.

Of all the conversations that Ava had over the years with coworkers, clients, and executives, the one with Cal the night she told him she was leaving for Cambridge was the worst one to date.

Although her decision meant leaving Cal behind, Ava knew it was the right move to help jump-start her life and eventually her career.

They tried to make it work long distance for a while, but their studies and a hardship took a toll on their relationship.

He came to visit once, but Ava convinced herself that ending things was the best thing to do. But to this day, Ava knew it was the biggest regret of her life.

Continuing to reminisce over pictures, Ava caught a glimpse of Shelby standing in the doorway.

"You and Cal were one of a kind," Shelby said, pausing for a minute. "Two peas in a pod. It seemed like nothing could break you two apart." Shelby could see the pain in Ava's eyes.

"Yeah, we were really something. Two kids, foolishly in love," said Ava as she let out a heavy sigh.

To provide a distraction, Shelby asked Ava if she could run down to Dr. Griffin's office and fill the pain medication prescribed to her at the hospital.

Surprised by the sudden need for pain medicine, Ava became worried and asked her mom where she was experiencing pain or if she needed to go back to the hospital.

"Oh no, dear. But I would like to have the pain meds on hand just in case. I'll be fine by myself. Please just head out now so we can enjoy our evening."

Ava, confident that Shelby was feeling okay, grabbed her purse and the prescription, and headed out to the doctor's office.

Ava was always amazed how small towns operate. In New York, she would need to call ahead and provide at least an hour for the pharmacist to get everything in order.

But here, she simply went into the doctor's office, and they offered it right there on the spot without waiting.

There were just some things that couldn't replace southern charm and the luxury of a small town, Ava thought.

Opening the door to the doctor's office and pharmacists, Ava listened to the clank of the door charm overhead. It reminded her of when she was little and would visit the doctors.

All of a sudden, Ava heard, "Well, look at you. All grown up! Come here and give me a hug." Caroline Andy was the receptionist at the doctor's office and one of Shelby's best friends.

"Hi, Caroline. I didn't know you worked here," Ava said. "It's so good to see you. How have you been?"

"Oh, honey, I've been good. How are you doing? To receive a call like that about your mom must have given you a fright. I can't even imagine. Is she feeling better?"

Caroline always had a calming sense about her that made you want to open up and tell her everything. Her genuine personality made it easy to talk with her.

"She's feeling much better. Thanks for asking. Almost back to her old self, wanting to make plans, cook up a feast, relax on the patio, and talk for hours," Ava said, smiling.

"That's so good to hear, Ava. Well, if you two need anything or a home-cooked meal, please let me know, and I'll bring it right on over," Caroline said warmly. "How long will you be staying this trip?"

"I'm not sure just yet. Certainly until Mom gets back on her feet and able to get along without me," Ava said.

"That's good to hear, dear." And then with a twinkle in her eye, she asked if Ava was waiting to see the doctor.

"I'm not sure. I just need a prescription filled. Do you need to see the doctor for that, or can you just take care of it?" Ava inquired.

"Oh, you should wait for the doctor. I think it would be best for you to see him, especially with your mom's condition.

You never know when prescriptions may need a consultation for hospitalized patients," Caroline said with a playful smile.

Ava, obviously missing the undertone of Caroline's response, politely accepted her request and sat down in the sitting area to wait for the doctor.

8

Reading through the tabletop magazines, Ava looked up at the little girl sitting across from her. Her blond hair dangled in front of her flush face, indicating she didn't feel well.

The young child clung to her mother's side as if her mom had a power that would instantly make her feel better.

As Ava began reliving her own memories of her visits to the same doctor's office, she looked up to hear the internal door opening.

Right then, as if time had never elapsed, Cal walked out of the doorway with a patient. Her heart stopped, but in a good way this time.

He had aged well. She took notice of his broad shoulders and jet-black hair.

His eyes were still a mesmerizing blue with a hint of green, and he had eyelashes that went on for days. She remembered them being captivating to stare into when they were younger.

His height allowed him to tower over people, but his humbling demeanor made him so approachable that he never met a stranger.

Ava watched in awe as he carried himself in conversation. His intellect shined through the more he spoke, but his slight southern voice made Ava melt inside. There is just something about a man who was as genuine as he spoke.

He was as impressive as she remembered.

In disbelief that Cal had become a doctor, let alone was her mother's doctor, Ava froze in her seat. His grace and ease in his element really made him even more attractive, if that was possible.

As if in slow motion, Cal turned his head and paused a moment, simply staring at Ava before managing to steadily say, "Ava, it's been a long time."

Walking over to her as she rose from her seat, Cal never took his eyes off Ava. His smile was still genuine but appeared more mature than the boy Ava remembered.

His baby blues still burned a hole right through Ava, making her feel vulnerable and on display. The attraction between the two had not fizzled as their relationship had so many years ago.

Greeting Ava warmly, Cal embraced her with a strong, long-lasting hug that made Ava weak in the knees. "Hi, Cal," Ava said in a faint whisper in his ear. "It's good to see you." Ava smiled sweetly. Shooting a look to Caroline who was peering at them from her desk, Ava said, "I didn't realize you were Shelby's primary care physician. I assume you know about her stroke?"

"She didn't tell you I was her physician?" Cal snickered as Ava shook her head, beginning to realize her mother intended her to see Cal again. "Maybe she thought you wouldn't come if you knew I was the doctor in town."

Starting to see that Ava was becoming annoyed at the lack of full disclosure, Cal, like a switch, turned from a coy boyhood friend to a professional doctor.

"Yes, I did know that Shelby had suffered what appears to be a stroke. It was my understanding she was under the care of Dr. Sophie. Is that correct?"

Taken aback by Cal's assertiveness, an attribute Ava had only seen a few times when they were growing up, Ava stammered, "Well…yes. That's correct."

"Ava, Dr. Sophie is an exceptional doctor who is more than qualified to handle your mother's condition. From her charts, she appears to have come out of the coma nicely and is recovering wonderfully. Although I do want to see her in my office in one week for a follow-up, there is nothing to indicate a hindrance in her recovery."

A sigh of relief came over Ava, and her eyes began to sting with tears. Cal reached for Ava's shoulder and comforted her in a way most others could not. "Ava, it will be okay," he said in a deep, husky voice that was soothing. "Your mom will make it through this. She is a fighter. Just like you."

Looking up at him, there were no words to describe the impact that phrase meant to Ava at that exact moment.

She flung her arms around Cal and squeezed him so tight; she didn't want to let go. A simple thank-you was all she said.

They separated from each other and Cal uttered, "Shelby's prescriptions can be picked up next door at the pharmacy. Our buildings are connected, so you can walk down this hallway, and you'll see Stan on the other side."

"Stan? Stan Berling? From high school?" Ava questioned emphatically.

"Yes, he started working for me a few years ago when he and his family moved back from the West Coast."

"Wow, what a small world. And you, Cal. You became a doctor," Ava said, although she wasn't surprised.

Cal was the type of man who could accomplish anything he wanted.

"Yes, ma'am, I did. And don't play coy with me, Miss Stillman. A highly successful businesswoman in the big city, renowned for her shrewd negotiating skills with high-profile clients," Cal said with a hint of cleverness to his voice.

Smirking in disbelief, Ava said, "Yes, how did you know?"

Pausing for a moment to put the pieces together and figure out how Cal knew of her accomplishments. "Oh, right, Mom is best friends with your assistant. Got it!"

Trying to move the conversation along, Ava thanked him for the information, and Cal mentioned that if Shelby needed more scripts filled before he saw her again in a week that we could simply call.

Oh yeah, why didn't I think of that? Next time, Ava thought to herself as she made a mental note.

"I'll remind my mother of that. Wait, if you are her doctor, why weren't you at the hospital with her when she needed you?"

The statement probably came off harsher than intended, but it reminded Ava of when they broke things off. Ava toyed with the idea that maybe he didn't love her as she thought, since he didn't fight for the relationship.

But before Ava fell deeper into a tailspin of emotion, Cal interrupted her thoughts. "I was there when your mom was first brought into the hospital. My rounds had just ended. Don't worry. I wasn't leaving her to fend for herself. We have a great group of doctors at our practice, and she was in good hands."

Letting out a sigh of relief, Ava was physically and emotionally drained.

"Thank you, Cal. I'm certain you are an outstanding doctor, but when it comes to my mom, I'm just a little overprotective, especially since Dad passed away."

"Yeah, I was very sorry to hear of your family's loss, Ava. If I wouldn't have been completing my residency, I would have come back to pay my respects. He was a wonderful man who helped so many. I feel like I learned so much from him over the years."

With a tender heart, Ava nodded and accepted Cal's terms of endearment. They parted ways and agreed to meet again when Ava brought Shelby in for her appointment.

As Ava walked away, she began thinking what kind of life Cal must have and how happy he seemed.

9

"Mom!" Ava shouted as she came through the front door. "Why didn't you tell me that Cal was your doctor? That was not a nice joke. Mom, where are you?"

A fleeting moment of panic struck Ava's chest when Shelby didn't answer, but then there was a faint clanking sound coming from the kitchen.

Ava headed toward the back of the house and found her mother listening to music and starting to make dinner, which was something she loved to do.

"Mom, did you hear me come in the house?" Ava said, looking for a response from Shelby.

"Oh, hi, honey. How was the doctor? Any trouble with the prescription?" Shelby said with a smirk on her face.

"Very funny. Why didn't you tell me Cal was your doctor?"

"Would you have wanted to go pick up the prescription if you knew?"

"I don't know, but I would have if you needed them."

"I know dear, but everyone deserves a nice surprise every now and again. And, Ava, you seemed so sad recalling all the good times you had with Cal that I thought it would be nice to see an old friend. Are you mad at me?" Shelby asked in all sincerity.

"No, Mom. I'm not mad," Ava said as she approached her standing by the counter. "How could I ever be mad at you? I love you too much."

They both giggled and embraced in a genuine hug.

"Now, let's make a scrumptious dinner. Shall we?" Shelby said with a look of whimsy. But they were interrupted by the doorbell.

Looking at each other, puzzled, Ava headed off to see who was at the door. It was Caroline with a warm meal in hand.

Caroline lifted up the casserole dish when Ava opened the door, saying, "Well, I mentioned bringing over a hot meal, so I thought tonight was as good as any."

Smiling brightly, Ava ushered Caroline in the house. "Mom, Caroline is here. She brought us a casserole for dinner."

Shelby came sprinting around the corner as best she could, eager to see her friend. "Caroline, it's great to see you. Thank you so much for coming over, but you didn't need to make such a fuss."

"Just stop it with all that talk," Caroline said waving her hand in the air. "You know I would have been here sooner if Ava wasn't here taking such great care of you."

Ava, attempting to give the two friends some time to chat and catch up, took the casserole dish and said, "Why don't you ladies relax outside with some cold ice tea, and I'll make our plates for dinner?"

"That sounds like a marvelous idea," Shelby said. The two trotted off to the chairs on the patio to catch up on the latest gossip.

Although Shelby was getting along well, Ava had her concerns that she might not be recovering as well as she was letting on to her.

While Ava was preparing the plates for dinner, she overheard Shelby and Caroline's conversation through the kitchen window.

"Were you scared, Shelby? I couldn't imagine what you thought when you woke up in a hospital," Caroline asked, very concerned.

"No, I wasn't scared," said Shelby. "I was confused, to tell you the truth. One minute I am preparing to go for my normal morning walk with Barbara, and the next thing I know, I felt dizzy. Silly me, I thought it was just because I was hungry, so I sat down. When I came to, I was in the hospital, and Ava was there. Sweet girl, coming all this way from New York and especially after everything she's been through lately," Shelby said with sadness in her expression.

"What do you mean?" Caroline asked concerned.

Before Shelby could answer, Ava quickly jutted to the screen door and asked if they were ready for dinner and where they wanted to eat—inside or out on the patio.

Bringing their food to the rickety old picnic table outside, which had so many wonderful memories, Ava was prepared to eat and not talk or hear about New York.

The three of them had great stories to share. Caroline explained how Cal had taken over the Tilks' family business when Mr. Tilk retired. She went on to say that Cal had saved everyone's job that worked for Tilk.

She even explained how he volunteered a few days a month at the local shelter to help families in need who didn't have health insurance.

Shelby spoke about how she had been keeping busy with her friends, exercising, and having activity nights down at the lodge. She went on about the new dance lessons and group outings to see local attractions.

Ava mentioned that work was going great, and she was in the midst of closing a huge merger with two family-cultured companies.

Although mergers could be difficult, Ava was optimistic about these two organizations coming together because they both truly valued their employees, which was a rarity in any industry.

After dinner, Shelby was tired and hoped to enjoy a good night's sleep.

Ava walked Caroline to the door and thanked her tremendously for coming over this evening. "It's been great catching up with you, Caroline, and I know it meant a lot to Mom having you here tonight."

"Dear, it's been my pleasure. Your mom is such a good friend," Caroline said. "If I may, I know you and Cal were close in high school. I don't know if you have the time while you're back, but I'm sure he would enjoy spending some time with you. He works so hard, and he's such a good man. He deserves to have some fun and catch up with an old friend."

Giggling at the idea, Ava said, "Thank you, Caroline, for the thought, but I don't think his wife would take too kindly to his high school girlfriend wanting to hang out for old times' sake."

Caroline, making a dash to her car since the wind had picked up, turned around, and with an artful response, said,

"Ava, what makes you think this is anything more than two friends catching up on lost time?" Ava hesitated before her response but was cut off by Caroline, "Plus, who said Cal was married?"

With a twinkle in her eye, Caroline got in her car, and a smile beamed across Ava's face.

She was unsure why the idea of learning Cal wasn't married was intriguing to her, but nevertheless, it was a delightful surprise.

10

The next morning, Ava awoke to the sun sparkling across her yellow-and-blue bedspread with birds chirping out her window.

"So Cal isn't married, huh," Ava said with happiness filling her inside. *Well, perhaps we could get together for coffee, for old times' sake, like Caroline said,* Ava thought to herself.

Since it was so early in the morning, Ava thought she would run out to get bagels for herself and her mom to have when Shelby woke up for the day.

Making her way into Sweetums Bakery and Fresh Goods, Ava spotted some delicious, fresh blueberry muffins. The sugar crystals on top glistened from the sunlight coming in the bay window, and the blueberries smelled delectable and fresh.

As Ava filled her box full of mouthwatering breakfast delights, she also saw chocolate chip muffin tops, like her father used to make.

Taking in the whiff of the chocolate, she was immediately taken back to her kitchen as a young child.

She saw her dad in the kitchen, whipping up a batch of his famous muffin tops. Ava usually offered to help him bake but secretly wanted to taste test the chocolate. Those were fond memories that Ava treasured.

Ava rounded the corner to account for a few bagels, the main reason for coming to Sweetums, and she accidently bumped into someone standing directly beside the rack of candy. They splashed all over the floor.

"Oh, I am so sorry, sir. I didn't even see you there," Ava said, bending down to pick up the candy.

"Ava?" a man's voice said inquisitively. "What are you doing up so early?"

Frozen in her stooped position, Ava peered upward, only to find Cal standing in front of her. "Cal! What... Me... Oh, I'm getting breakfast for Mom and me."

"The Ava I knew wouldn't get up before noon, let alone seven in the morning," Cal said jokingly.

"Yeah, well, things are different. We aren't teenagers anymore."

"Yes, I remember," Cal said, returning Ava's box of breakfast goods to her.

"Thank you. I'm sorry I bumped into you," Ava said.

Trying to muster up the courage to ask Cal for coffee, Cal said, "Well, hey, listen, I have to run to the office. Patients like to see me early before they go to work. It was great seeing you again."

With Cal ending the conversation so abruptly, she wondered if he was still hurt from their breakup after so many years had passed.

Taking a leap of faith, Ava decided to grab some gumption and blurted out, "Cal, I was wondering if you had some time later. Perhaps we could meet for lunch or an afternoon coffee?"

As he reached the door, he turned to hear the last part of Ava's question. With a serious look in his eyes, one Ava had seen before, he said, "Lunch could be hectic, and I have rounds this afternoon at the hospital."

"Oh, okay. Another time then before I head back to New York," Ava responded and turned back toward the counter.

"Ava," Cal said as the door opened and the bells at the top chimed. She quickly turned around to meet his face. "I'm free for dinner if you are."

She smiled at Cal, and he took that as a sign of acceptance. "Great, I'll pick you up at your mom's house around eight."

Thinking about what she would wear, butterflies began to form in her stomach. She was so consumed with tonight's plan that she didn't hear the cashier the first few times she said what the total was for her breakfast order.

When Ava returned to the house, she saw her mom at the breakfast nook, drinking coffee and reading the paper. "Oh, excellent, you're up!"

"Well, of course I am, dear. It's nearly eight. Where did you head out to this morning? I half expected you to be sleeping until noon today," Shelby said.

Ava laughed. "Why does everybody still think I sleep in until noon?"

Shelby looked at Ava, confused. "Everybody, dear? Who's everybody?"

"When I went into town for breakfast, I saw Cal at Sweetums Bakery," Ava said as she pulled out the freshly baked goods.

Whiffing in the amazing smells, Shelby said "Ohhh, what did you get? It smells heavenly."

She paused as if pretending not to have heard what Ava said. But then when Ava didn't continue, Shelby motioned her hands and said, "So you saw Cal. And? How did that go?"

Playing right into Shelby's response, Ava stated, "I got us a smorgasbord of blueberry muffins, chocolate chip muffin tops, and an assortment of bagel flavors with a few options for cream cheese."

"Thanks, sweetheart. This smells wonderful, but you still didn't answer my question."

"It was good to see Cal. Crazy that we bumped into each other, but we did decide to meet up for dinner tonight. Unless of course you need me here, then I can just reschedule or postpone. Or, Mom, would you mind if we just had dinner here?"

A twinkle in her mom's eye, Shelby said excitedly, "Here? Well, that would be great! We could all make dinner together if you'd like. Or if you two want to be alone, I understand."

"Mom, it's not like that. Hopefully, we can be friends. After all the good times we had together when I was growing up, why wouldn't he want to hang out? It's not like we're dating. I'm hoping he still wants to be friends after everything I put him through."

Shelby looked at Ava, wishing she could see what Shelby saw when she looked at her: a sweet and kind person. And that all Cal wanted more than anything was to be with her and to treat her how she deserved.

"Ava, I'm certain he wants to be friends, if not more."

"Mother!" Ava said loudly. "I highly doubt that. Plus, logistically, it wouldn't even make sense."

"Sometimes love doesn't, sweetheart. Sometimes it just all works out the way it was meant to, whether it makes sense to us at the time or not."

Ava loved how simple her mother could put things into perspective. She was amazing at turning a complicated situation into a simple understanding with a few words. It was her gift.

They each enjoyed their delicious breakfast as they had a little bit of everything.

* * *

Later that day, Ava was preparing some notes for work when she received an e-mail from Jackie.

> Ava,
>
> My sympathies with your mother's condition. I hope she recovers soon and is back to herself.
>
> Thank you for sending along the copies of the changes to the contract for the Parker, Stokes, Addison, and Associates merger. As always, outstanding work!
>
> I also appreciate you telecommuting while you are taking care of your mother. Please advise when you will be returning so we can wrap up this merger and move on to the next.
>
> Regards,
> Jackie

Really, she has the gall to e-mail me as if nothing happened? Ava thought to herself. Letting out her frustrations, Ava attempted to maintain her professionalism and keep her composure while responding to her e-mail.

Jackie,

Thank you for your kind words. I appreciate your position when it comes to my mother.

Yes, once I receive the paperwork back from both clients, I will be sending them over for the final meeting to sign and complete this package.

I plan to return to work in a few weeks, barring my mother's condition continues to improve and not worsen as per my e-mail to HR prior to my departure. Should my plans change, I will advise accordingly.

Ava

Letting out a deep breath, Ava felt a sigh of relief. *There, now, I can get back to work,* Ava thought to herself.

After a few hours of due diligence, making sure everything was ready to go for the merger, Ava looked up to see time had escaped her.

It was nearing seven in the evening, and she still needed to get ready and plan dinner for when Cal arrived.

Thinking of what she had packed in her suitcase, she realized there was nothing that would be a casual summer dress for an unexpected evening with an ex-boyfriend that you regrettably broke up with years ago.

Deciding on a secondary plan, Ava headed toward her closet in hopes of finding the perfect dress for such an occasion.

Ava sorted through several options before landing on a cream-colored, sleeveless sundress with pink baby rosebuds meshed into the fabric, tailored with a thin lace neckline.

With Ava's tan skin remaining from her rooftop lunches at work, the cream would really look good and give Ava the confidence she needed to get through the evening.

Ava headed out to the main room to find Shelby reading a book in her chair. Shelby looked up. "Wow, Ava, you look lovely. Are you sure this is just a friendly get together?"

They both giggled, and Ava said, "Yes, Mom, I'm sure. I saw this in the closet and thought why not. I didn't bring any dresses with me when I packed."

"All right then," Shelby said. "Now, what shall we make for dinner?"

Heading into the kitchen, they thought of a fun meal where they could all participate and gather around the island like old times. "What about shish kebabs? I have all the ingredients to make them. I even have fresh vegetables in the garden out back."

"That sounds great, Mom. Thanks," Ava said.

The doorbell rang, and they both jumped. Shelby could see Ava's heart almost leaping out of her chest in excitement and panic at the same time.

"It will be fine, sweetheart. He's just a boy in a man's body. Right now, he doesn't remember that you broke his heart. All he is thinking about is rekindling the friendship you two once had. And as you said, logistically a relationship wouldn't be possible anyway. So stop worrying."

With the brutal but simple honesty, Ava was relieved.

What was she worried about? Soon, she would be heading back to New York, and Cal would be staying in Keokuk. This harsh reality settled Ava and grounded her nerves.

With a little less glee, Ava approached the front door and opened it to find Cal standing there, holding a single white rose.

Ava blushed and said, "Well, hello there, stranger. The rose is beautiful, but you shouldn't have."

"Well, hello to you too! This is actually for your mom. She always mentions how pretty the arrangements are in the office, so I thought I'd pick her one before heading over here. I hope that's okay," Cal said.

Feeling a bit embarrassed, Ava looked down at the floor as she ushered Cal inside. "I'm certain she will adore it. What woman doesn't love flowers?"

Passing by Ava to enter the house, Cal leaned in and whispered, "You. You don't like flowers."

Ava inhaled sharply, and her heart started pounding. She couldn't believe that Cal remembered something so little.

"Unless something has changed, you prefer chocolates and little notes—one to melt in your mouth and the other to melt your heart."

Taking a step back, Cal stared deep into Ava's eyes.

In that moment, Ava was thankful to be holding on to the door as her legs began to shake from his intense baby-blue eyes.

Cal's eyes always had an effect on Ava. It was amazing to think after all this time, their chemistry still existed.

Shelby appeared around the corner, breaking the intense moment. She embraced Cal in a big hug, welcoming him into her home.

"Dr. Michaels, it's so good to see you," Shelby said.

"Shelby, please call me Cal. You're like a second mom to me," Cal said. "And this is for you."

"Oh, what a sweet gesture. Thank you so much. I know I can call you Cal, but it is fun to call the boy who practically lived at your house years ago 'doctor.'" Shelby chuckled. "Well, come on in, and let's get started."

"Started? Sure, okay. I'm game. What are we doing?"

"Oh yeah, sorry. I told Mom we'd stay here and make dinner with her. I hope that's all right," Ava said, regretting that she hadn't had the opportunity to tell Cal sooner.

"That's perfect. I love to cook. What are we whipping up this evening?" Cal said enthusiastically.

Ava was surprised by his passion to cook. She realized there was much that occurred over the past ten years that they might not know about each other.

As they all entered the kitchen, Shelby said, "Shish kebabs!"

"That sounds excellent. I'm a mean griller," Cal said as they all laughed.

11

The evening progressed with stories about the last ten years. Ava couldn't remember the last time she had such fun not worrying about work or Eric.

Even the thought of his name made Ava's skin crawl. She hated herself for even thinking about him at a time like this.

Preparing the dinner was a lighthearted occasion. Cal and Ava shared a bottle of wine as Shelby sipped on her fruit-infused water.

"Mom, I wish you could have some of this wine. It's delicious," Ava said, continuing to take sips from her glass.

"I bet it is. I haven't seen you have a drink since you've been here. It must be good," Shelby said with a smirk. "Besides, what would my doctor say if he saw me drinking alcohol?"

Cal spoke up in a serious tone, "He'd probably say you're doing the right thing by staying hydrated. And no alcohol is a good rule of thumb until you are cleared at the two-week mark. But I must agree with you, Ava. I do like my summer blend. It has a punch of citrus flavor that can really go with any meal."

Shocked by Cal's response, Ava sarcastically responded, "Wait, you make wine now too? Geez, is there anything you can't do Doctor Michaels?"

Cal paused and looked at Ava intently before answering, "As a matter of fact, yes, there are a few things I can't do. I just don't care to admit them." They all chuckled.

With a quick grin, Cal went on to say that he learned to make wine when he took up his love for cooking. He found it to be therapeutic to make his own wine.

"Well, when I tasted it before, I thought it was delicious," Shelby said. "Why do you think I keep buying them from you, Cal?"

Cal smiled as he picked up the plate of prepared shish kebabs and headed outside toward the grill.

Shelby looked at Ava. "Honey, I'm going to sit in the living room and relax until dinner is ready. Why don't you keep Cal company outside, and let me know when we're ready to eat."

"Are you sure, Mom? Are you not feeling well?" Ava asked, concerned.

"Oh, no, I'm fine. Just wanting to rest a little before we eat," Shelby said as she trailed off to the living room.

Ava hated seeing her mom not fully back to her peppy self, but all things considered, she thought Shelby was doing amazingly well.

However, Ava's waves of anxiety soon fell over her as she realized she and Cal would be alone. She took to liquid courage, filled up her glass with more wine, and headed outside.

Handing Cal his glass, Ava said, "Here you go. I hear wine goes better with…well, everything."

As Cal began grilling, Ava looked out over the lake and said, "So many good memories here."

"I know. It seems like yesterday when we were here with your family, grilling out, making s'mores, and fishing. But look at us now. You're a successful businesswoman in New York City, and I'm a doctor. It's amazing the different paths life had in store for us," Cal said, trailing off with his words.

"Yes, indeed. I think it's great that you became a doctor, Cal. You really seem to shine in your element. You're a natural," Ava said, peering back at him over the rim of her glass. "You're staring," Ava said, blushing.

Cal couldn't take his eyes off Ava. "I'm sorry, I can't help myself. I always wondered what it would be like to see you again after we broke up."

"Oh, I knew it. Here it comes. Okay, just get it over with. I'm a terrible person. Selfish, cruel, and unkind to everyone I love," Ava said, grueling.

"Whoa, I didn't say all that," Cal said as he walked toward Ava.

"Yes, I was hurt, Ava, for a very long time because I couldn't make sense of what you had done to me, to us. At least, I couldn't at the time."

Ava, surprised by his last few words, drew her eyes upward to find Cal standing a few inches away from her.

She could smell his natural scent that used to linger in her car, on her clothes, and in her room. She felt a lump in her throat. Not sure what to make of the moment, Ava stammered out, "What do you mean 'at the time'?"

Slowly lifting his hand to her face, Cal caressed Ava's cheek ever so gently. "Ava. I've never stopped loving you, but I understand why you did what you did. It wasn't what I wanted at the time, but I completely understand."

"You were focused on your school and where you wanted to be in your career. But I only ever saw you. I couldn't see past you. It didn't make sense. So in a way, I guess I have you to thank for me becoming a doctor."

"Wait," Ava said defensively. "Are you saying that if I hadn't broken up with you, you would never have pursued your career as a doctor? You would have never helped others?"

"Oh, I think I would have ended up in a profession where I helped others, but I would have followed you anywhere, Ava. You were my world. My everything," Cal said intently.

Taking a minute to let the information sink in, Ava didn't respond. *Could he be telling the truth,* Ava wondered.

Ava pulled away from Cal and looked out over the lake. "Cal, I can never tell you how sorry I am that I ended things. I thought it was the best thing to do at the time. I wanted to focus on school, and being so far away from each other was incredibly difficult."

"Ava, no one said long-distance relationships were easy. But don't you think the good times outweighed the bad ones?" Cal said.

"Of course they did. But we were so young. Just out of high school, starting college, and miles away from each other," Ava said, trying to convince herself once again that what she had done nearly ten years ago was still the right decision.

Cal opened the grill to check the shish kebabs and then walked over to where Ava was standing. "Do you still think it was the right decision? Would you change anything knowing what you know now?"

Ava turned around to find Cal standing next to her once again. "Honestly, no. I wouldn't change that we broke up," Ava said with a heavy heart.

"I don't want you to think I am cruel, but, Cal, had we not broken up, you yourself said that you wouldn't have become a doctor. I wouldn't want to have deprived you and the world of such a wonderful gift. You are amazing at what you do."

"Thank you, Ava. That's sweet of you to say," Cal said, turning away.

"But I would take back breaking your heart—and mine, for that matter. I wish there would have been a way for both of us to achieve our careers, what we love doing, and be together."

Cal stepped forward and said, "Maybe there still is."

Silence fell between the two of them as they gazed into each other's eyes.

Just as Ava was going to speak, Shelby opened the screen door and asked if dinner was nearly ready as she was getting hungry.

With an aching silence shared between them and a longing in each other's eyes, no words were uttered. After what seemed like an eternity, Ava broke their connection and answered Shelby.

"Certainly, Mom. Why don't I come help put together the sides? I think Cal is nearly done," Ava said as she walked toward Shelby.

"Yes, Shelby. The grilling is nearly complete. Just a few more minutes until this delicious feast is ready," Cal said, never taking his gaze off Ava, hoping she would turn around to give him a sign.

Ava stepped into the kitchen to find the sides already prepped. "Mom, I thought we were going to prepare the sides together. They are already done?"

"Sweetheart, it sounded like it was getting intense out there. Are you all right?" Shelby said, concerned.

"Mom, I'm fine. Just rehashing what could have been between Cal and me. That's all."

"Okay, honey. I'm just worried about you, especially with the whole Eric situation. You are my little girl, and I still worry. No matter if you are three or thirty-three," Shelby said as she embraced Ava in a hug.

Without realizing it, Cal was standing behind her at the screen door. Ava was uncertain if he heard Shelby's comment about Eric, but he didn't seem to lead on as though he heard anything out of the ordinary.

The three of them sat down at the family dinner table, shared a pleasant meal, told stories, and reminisced about Cal and Ava's youth.

12

Ava walked Cal to his car and handed him a plate of leftovers. "I'm not certain why Mom constantly makes a to go plate, but I guess she has ever since you were a teenager," Ava said as she handed Cal his doggy bag.

Cal grabbed the door to his truck and said, "Ava, who is Eric?"

Ava froze and didn't know how to respond. Cal could see her pale face and saddened demeanor.

"I'm sorry, Ava. I didn't mean to upset you. I just over-heard your mother's comment. Is it something work-related or personal?"

Ava still didn't respond.

"Cal, do we have to talk about this right now?"

"No," he said with such certainty.

"We can discuss it tomorrow evening over dinner if you'd prefer. Or you can tell me now, and we can still go to dinner tomorrow evening. I'm guessing from your reaction we would have a better evening if we don't speak about Eric though."

Feeling lighthearted by Cal's response, Ava said, "All right then. Dinner tomorrow night it is."

"So do you want to talk about it now or later?" Cal said in a joking manner.

Ava looked down at her shoes and dug her foot into the dirt. "Oh boy, is it that bad?" Cal said.

Trying to figure out how she'd tell Cal that her boyfriend, who she thought was going to be her new husband, had actually been cheating on her with her boss the entire time they were together, Ava looked up, confused by Cal's response.

Cal pointed to Ava's foot, saying, "You always dig in your toes when there's a difficult topic you don't want to talk about, but you need to get out."

Ava laughed until Cal said, "I should know. It's what you would always do when you needed to tell me something big. It is how I knew something bad was happening the night that you ended things."

Irritated that Cal knew her so well, Ava began explaining to Cal about her relationship with Eric in a more frantic state of rambling than she had intended.

"Right before I received the call from the hospital about Mom, I had just walked in on my boyfriend, who I thought was going to propose soon, with my boss. Apparently, they had been seeing each other ever since Eric and I got together nearly a year ago. How stupid of me to think that I could end up happy, right?"

"Now, I am alone, feeling deceived, and trying to sort through the last year of my life, determining what were lies and what was the truth. Not to mention that I still work for this dreadful woman. I worked so hard for this company, and now I am forced to walk away from it because of them. I am so angry, upset, and hurt. I am a mess of emotions."

Ava chuckled to herself as a defense mechanism and said in a smart-alecky tone, "Aren't you glad you asked?"

Cal just stared at Ava as if he wanted to run up to her, embrace her, and tell her everything would work out just as God intended.

But he knew her all too well. Ava needed space and time so she could feel safe to love again.

"I'm sorry if you were expecting easy and uncomplicated. I'm sure you don't want to hear any of this, nor do you care."

Upset by the accusation, Cal said, "What makes you think I don't care, Ava? I would hope that we're still friends, and friends care about each other."

"I know. I guess I meant, after all this time and our conversation out on the patio… I just thought this would be the last thing you'd want to hear right now," Ava said, feeling overwhelmed.

"Really? The last thing I'd want to hear? Come on, Ava. I have a soul," Cal said. "I'm sorry to hear that Eric was such a jerk to you. I can't imagine what that must have been like to see them together. I'm always here to listen if you need me. But, Ava, remember you deserve better. You're a good person who, for some reason, got wrapped up with the wrong guy." With a boyish grin, Cal climbed up into his truck and said, "And if nothing else, I'm sure you let him have it. The Ava I knew wouldn't let that fly for a second."

Ava smirked and was relieved by his response. Pointing as his truck, Ava said, "I can't believe you still have this old thing."

"Hey, I have a lot of good memories with this truck," Cal said as Ava blushed. "Yeah, Dad and I worked for hours putting her back together over the years."

Ava, feeling embarrassed that she thought it was because they had their first kiss in his truck, said, "Yes, good times."

"Among other memories," Cal said as he started the truck. "I'll see you tomorrow for dinner. Good night, Ava."

"Good night, Cal," Ava said as she waved back.

That night, Ava thought endlessly of Cal and the words they exchanged together that night. She wondered what he meant by "Maybe there still is."

Ava allowed herself to drift off and dream of what a life with Cal would be like.

The intense chemistry clearly still existed between them, and he seems to have matured into a wonderful man. His boyish charm still existed though.

Thinking of what their lives could be like together, Ava began to get excited for the possibility of being with Cal. But then reality set in. She lived in New York City, and he lived in Keokuk.

No matter how close they seemed or might have once been, they were worlds apart. His life was there, and her life was miles away.

Again, she was faced with the same predicament. Brining herself back to reality, she convinced herself that nothing could happen between Cal. It just wouldn't work.

Feeling trapped and right back in the same place she was ten years ago, Ava decided to soak in a bubble bath before heading to bed.

The next morning, Ava awoke to the smell of maple pancakes and fresh orange juice. She walked to the kitchen and found Shelby waiting for her to wake up and join her for breakfast.

"Good morning!" Shelby said with a smile. "So how do you think last night went?"

"Mom, it went well. Amazing, in fact," Ava said, half asleep. "But there is no future with Cal. We live on two separate sides of the world. His life is here, and I wouldn't begin to ask him to move for me."

"Maybe he would want to move for you. You can't discount people, Ava. And you can't make a decision for them either. Would you ever consider moving closer to him?" Shelby said with a glimmer of hope.

Considering it seriously, Ava responded, "I don't know. I guess if there was an opening for someone in my line of work that was closer to him, I would consider it. But, Mom, he'd have to ask me first, and we are not even together that way."

"I see. So the flirtatious looks across the table and the long, serious talk outside was nothing. Is that what you're telling me?" Shelby asked.

"Well, I don't know if it was nothing, but we would certainly have a long way to go before one of us uproots what we've worked so hard to establish," Ava said, not sure who she was trying to convenience—herself or her mom.

Shelby laid her hand over her daughter's and said, "Ava, you have always been a strong, independent woman who could do anything she set her mind to, but try to remember that you are also a woman who deserves to be loved, respected, and cherished by someone who simply adores you. Your dad used to say that his goal every day when he woke up was to make me happy because when you love someone, you always want to see them happy. Not that you are responsible for someone else's happiness, but the joy you receive from making the one you love happy in turn makes you happy."

"Oh, Mom. You're going to make me cry. That's a beautiful love story," Ava said.

"Ava, what made it so special is that I woke up every day with the same idea. I just wanted to make him happy because if he was happy, I was happy. Ava, find a love that is true, and you'll find a love that lasts forever," Shelby said with a tender heart.

"You always know just want to say, Mom." Ava smiled.

"Now, before we get too serious so early in the morning, let's eat some pancakes."

13

Shelby began clearing the dishes as Ava finished her morning coffee. She sipped the vanilla goodness while looking out over the pond and seeing the mountains in the background. This view beat Ava's New York morning view any day.

Inhaling the richness to help kick start her day, Ava began planning how she would tackle her morning work schedule.

As her mind raced with all that she had to get done for the final paperwork on the merger, she heard the dishes crash in the sink.

Darting to Shelby, Ava saw the breakfast plates broken in the sink and her mom slumped over on the counter.

"Mom!" Ava exclaimed. "Mom, are you okay? What's wrong? Talk to me."

Shelby didn't respond right away, but her eyes wandered around to find Ava.

"Mom, talk to me. What happened?"

Shelby shook her head and grabbed her arm. "I'm not sure. I just got a little dizzy, that's all."

Ava, concerned, said, "The same dizziness you felt last time? Right before you fainted and had a stroke?"

"No, not exactly," Shelby said. "It was almost like I had too much sugar or something. Maybe some water and I can lie down. I'm sure I'll feel better soon."

Ava ran and got some water for her mom. Then she helped her to the chair in the living room and said, "I'm going to call Cal. Maybe he should check on you, or we should go to him?"

"I don't want to cause a fuss. I'm sure I'll be fine once I sit down and have some water," Shelby said, a little out of breath.

Shelby sat down in her recliner chair and seemed to regain some color in her face as she sipped on the water. Ava still wanted to call her doctor to make sure this wasn't a sign of something worse to come.

Sneaking out of the living room to grab her phone, Ava immediately began dialing Cal.

Three rings and Caroline picked up the phone. "Good morning, Dr. Griffin's office. This is Caroline speaking. How can I help you today?"

Frantically, Ava said, "Caroline, it's Ava. Mom just had a dizzy spell again. I'm worried this is an onset of something worse to come. Should we come in or go to the hospital?"

Ava was secretly wishing Caroline would just say to go to the hospital. She couldn't bear to see something happen to her mom. She couldn't lose her too.

"Ava, calm down, sweetie. Let me get Dr. Michaels, and he can best advise you. Hold on one minute, okay?" Caroline said in a composed, reassuring voice.

It seemed like ages before Cal picked up the phone, but it was merely seconds. "Ava, how's Shelby?"

"Oh, Cal. I'm not sure. She seemed fine all morning. We finished breakfast, and the next thing I knew I heard the clash of dishes in the sink. When I reached her, she was slumped over on the counter."

"Did she fall or lose consciousness? Was her speech slurred?"

Hearing Cal be so direct was a comforting feeling. He really had come into his own and found his calling.

Thinking back to this morning, Ava said, "No, neither. When I got to her, her eyes were open but seemed to struggle to find mine. But she was lucid. She did grab her arm though."

This answer didn't seem to trigger an alarm for Cal, but he still wanted to see her and make his own evaluation.

"Ava, is she in any condition to travel? I'd like to see her in my office. I'm not certain if this is related to what recently happened or something else."

"Let me see." When Ava walked back into the living room, Shelby was asleep in the chair.

Not wanting to wake her mom, she said, "Cal, she is asleep. Should I wake her and bring her in? Should she even be asleep right now? What if she goes into another coma?"

Clearly sensing that Ava was overwhelmed by her mother's condition, Cal said, "No, that's okay. I can be there in fifteen minutes. I will assess her and see if she needs to be admitted, but I don't think so from what you're telling me. Try to remain calm, and I'll be there shortly."

"Thanks, Cal. I'll see you soon."

When Cal arrived, Shelby was still sleeping in the chair, and Ava had quickly changed into jeans and a shirt so she was prepared just in case they were headed to the hospital.

As Cal approached the front door, Ava opened it before he could knock.

Without exchanging any words, she immediately ushered him over to where Shelby was resting.

Watching Cal check Shelby's vitals and evaluate her physical condition made Ava think that there might be more to the situation that Cal was letting on, but he kept his composure, which brought a sense of calm over Ava.

Startled awake, Shelby opened her eyes and, in a confused state, said, "What's going on? Cal, what are you doing here?"

"Well, it's good to hear that you know who I am," Cal said with a chuckle.

"Of course, I know who you are. Ava, why did you call Cal? I told you I was fine. If you wanted to see him so bad, you didn't need to use me as an excuse," Shelby said as she gave Ava an irritating grin.

"Mom, that's not why I called him. You scared me. I've never seen you keeled over like that, let alone go completely pale. Then you just wanted to lie down," Ava said as if she had to defend her answer.

Cal interrupted their discussion. "Shelby, Ava had every right to call me. She was worried about you, as she should be. You just suffered a minor stroke, and things like this are exactly why we don't send patients in your condition home by themselves unless there is someone there to look after them."

"I guess so, but I am perfectly fine, right?" Shelby said, throwing her hands around, irritated that she was being fussed over by anyone.

"Your vitals seem stable, and your color seems, well, quite vibrant," Cal said, looking down with a smirk, knowing the reason for her pinkness was the irritation of Ava calling him.

"Thank you, Dr. Michaels," Shelby said as she gave Ava a hard stare. "See, Ava, I am fine. Now, I am going to lie down in my room for some peace and quiet. I will meet you out here a little later, and we can do lunch. I know you have to work, Ava."

Shelby sauntered off to her bedroom and yelled back, "Thank you again for coming, Cal! See you this evening." Shelby closed the door loudly.

"I'm so sorry, Cal, for calling when I didn't need to. She's full of piss and vinegar, it seems. I've just never seen her like that before," Ava said, seemingly shaken.

"It's okay, Ava," Cal said as he packed up his medical bag. "Seeing a loved one experience an episode and not knowing exactly what it means can be frightening." He placed his hand on Ava's arm to comfort her. "She is a fighter and seems to be in good spirits. Albeit having her daughter call the doctor on her," Cal said, smiling.

"Okay, okay. Not you too," Ava said.

Not meaning to leave in haste, Cal gathered the rest of his things and headed for the front door.

"I'm sorry to rush out, but I do have other patients waiting on me. I didn't know how long I would be gone, but I asked Caroline to reschedule until I could return to the office."

"Oh, I understand. Yes, please go. And, Cal, thank you so much for coming to make sure Mom was okay," Ava said with bright eyes and all sincerity.

"Anything for my patients, Ava. But you are certainly welcome." Cal turned and sprinted out to his truck.

As he pulled away, he hollered out that he would see her later that night for dinner.

14

Before Ava allowed herself to get swept up thinking about her evening with Cal, she focused on making sure Shelby felt better and completing some necessary items for work.

She popped her head into Shelby's room to check on her, and she was fast asleep in her bed. Ava brought her another bottle of water and pulled the covers up to make her as comfortable as possible.

As Ava looked at her mother, she couldn't imagine a day when she wasn't there. Although it was inevitable one day that her mother would pass, Ava prayed that it would be a long time from that moment.

Settling in to her old desk, she sent off an e-mail to Carol-Ann in human resources and copied Jackie, advising them that she would need to work remote a bit longer as her mother had an unexpected setback in her recovery.

Although it was still out of character to be including HR in her responses rather than just to Jackie, Ava did not want anything to be misconstrued as though she wasn't doing her job.

If Jackie was sly and cunning enough to sleep with her boy-friend for a year without her realizing it, who knows what else she was capable of doing.

Ava worried that her time away from the office would give Jackie reason to fire her, but she hoped that with her tenure at the company and movement she had made with upper management and clients, there wouldn't be an opportunity for Jackie to sabotage her professionally.

Regardless of the outcome, Ava was happy to be home and able to help her mom get back on her feet. Even though it seemed like she might not need it, Ava was concerned that Shelby felt worse that she let others believe.

Sorting through her inbox and the hundreds of e-mails that had come in over the past few days, Ava realized she still needed to respond to Addison regarding the requested changes to the proposal package and then have Parker and Stokes countersign the addendum.

Ava recalled Addison requesting changes be made to the succession planning section.

Since she was aware of both companies' goals with the merger, Ava wrote in her recommendation on the addendum and supplied a rationale in her response to Mark.

Mark,

My apologies for the delayed response in your desired alterations to the agreement. My mother, who we thought was getting better, had a setback this morning. We are recuperating well and expecting a recovery, but it is slow moving.

Anyway, I did have a moment to make some adjustments and add it to the addendum that Parker and Stokes already signed. Recognizing the importance of both companies is its employees, I'm offering the following suggestion to the 3.1 section of "Succession Planning."

Section 3.1: Succession Planning for Parker, Stokes, Addison, and Associates

As it relates to the continuation of employment for employees of Parker and Stokes and Addison Associations on the date of merger, all employees will maintain their existing position and pay as it was on the date of the merger.

No employee shall lose their working status with the newly formed company as long as they continue to perform their duties as outlined by both firms prior to the merger.

In the first thirty days after the merger, all positions within the company will be evaluated for most efficient use of time, talent, and effectiveness.

Once all jobs have been reviewed, human resources, along with Parker, Stokes, and Addison, will assess any duplication, possible promotions, and desire of position movement within the company from each employee.

Employees who have more than one year of tenure are eligible to apply for new positions that were created from the first thirty-day evaluation period.

No employee shall be declined a position, new or existing, solely on the basis of prior company affiliation.

An annual review will allow the company adequate time to determine where their employees stand with success, areas for improvement, and/or termination.

The length of time between the opportunity to stay in an employee's given position or elevate to a new position should be no longer than twelve months.

All employees who were employed at the time of the merger and remain employed after the first year will receive a 5 percent bonus on the anniversary of the two companies merging as a thank you for staying with the company and helping the organization thrive.

Mark, I hope the above addresses your retention concerns. From my perspective, it is a great way to keep all employees, guarantee employment while still allowing the company to grow once merged, as well as share some of the profits with those that stay with the company.

Please review the above and advise of any additional changes to this addendum. If approved, I will forward your signed copy over to Parker and Stokes for their countersigning of the changes.

Once the above is completed, we will be on our way to becoming Parker, Stokes, Addison, and Associates.

Thank you,
Ava Stillman
VP of Strategic Partnerships
Truman Partners

Being pleased with her crafted appendix, Ava decided that she would wait for Mark's response. If he agreed to the proposed agreement change, then she would forward along to Parker and Stokes.

Ava was hopeful that this would be the final piece to solidifying the deal. Once it was settled, she had every intention of putting in her two weeks' notice and finding another job.

She couldn't bear to work for Jackie one second longer than absolutely necessary.

Taking a break from work, Ava checked in on her mom. She was still sound asleep, so Ava decided to make some lunch before waking Shelby from her peaceful nap.

15

"Ava, dear, you're going to be late!" Shelby shouted from the living room.

Ava rolled her eyes as she always did when she was irritated at the utterance of something obvious. "I know, Mom. I'm hurrying as much as I can. You know there's nothing wrong if Cal waits five minutes for me. I'm sure he would understand!" Ava stated, still screaming, even though she was walking down the hall toward the living room.

As she looked up from her purse at her mother to continue on the never-ending rant, she realized Cal had already arrived and was waiting in the living room for her.

"Oh, Cal, I didn't know you were here. I'm sorry," Ava said, looking over at Shelby.

"I don't know if I would look too hard at Shelby." Cal chuckled. "She did say that you would be late."

With a sassy look and realization that she was out of line, Ava simply looked at Cal and said, "Well, would you still like to go to dinner, or shall we wait here and discuss a little more about how late I am?"

"Oh, Ava, learn to laugh in the moment even if it's at yourself," Shelby said as she brushed off her daughter's attitude.

"Yes, Mother," Ava said as she walked over to give her a hug and kiss.

"Now, you're sure you are feeling okay?" Ava said, concerned. "No dizziness or headaches?"

Shelby shook her head, "No, I am fine. You kids go have a good night and stop worrying about me. I am as healthy as I'll ever be."

"All right, well, I made some ziti for you if you get hungry. It's in the kitchen. And I won't be gone long. It's just dinner, but please call if you need me," Ava said with a hint of concern in her voice.

"Thank you, dear. Ziti sounds delicious," Shelby said, trying to be compliant to get Ava out the door.

Ava turned to Cal and ushered him to the door. "See you later, Mom."

"Bye, sweetie. Bye, Cal. Have a nice evening," Shelby said as she got up and headed toward the kitchen.

Cal walked Ava to his truck and opened the car door. Ava had almost forgotten the little niceties that true gentlemen did for women. She couldn't remember the last time Eric had opened a car door for her.

Normally, the city was so busy that people rushed into the Ubers without giving a second thought to chivalrous manners.

On the way to the restaurant, Ava began to worry that she shouldn't be having dinner with Cal so soon after Eric.

He was someone she wanted to spend the rest of her life with a week ago, but Cal was at one point too.

Ava struggled inside with how she should feel and how she actually felt. Lost in her own train of thought, she didn't realize Cal had turned on the radio.

A familiar song played softly through the speakers, "I Never Told You." Ava's lips parted, and her breath was taken away.

The song that she listened to on repeat for months after she ended it with Cal in college was playing on the radio. What were the odds?

Ava's college roommate begged her to play something else as it started to make her depressed just listening to it so much. But Ava couldn't help thinking that every word struck a nerve with Ava.

After the breakup, Ava missed Cal so much. There were many restless nights and sporadic moments when Ava wanted to drive all night to rush back into Cal's arms, if he would have her. But she never went after him, and he didn't come after her.

In hindsight, Ava wished they could have stayed together and made it work; but if she had, Cal wouldn't have become the amazing doctor that he was today.

As the song finished its last line "I miss everything about you, without you," Cal said, "You know this song has real merit."

"You think so?" Ava said, attempting to remain calm and not let her emotion come pouring through.

Cal pulled into the parking lot of the restaurant and put the truck in park. "Yeah, it's like it's saying everything I can't put into words."

Ava listened to Cal's words intently while hearing the pounding of her heart, praying he couldn't hear it too.

Cal reached out his hand to turn Ava's face toward him. "Ava, I know we are coming here tonight as old friends catching up, but I can't say that seeing you again hasn't brought up some lingering feelings."

Ava, still speechless, tried to utter something, anything, but nothing would come out. She simply couldn't think of what to say.

Cal lifted his arm to put on the headrest behind Ava and leaned in closer.

She could smell his earthy cologne and sweet natural scent. To her, it hadn't changed since they were younger.

Ava inhaled sharply, trying not to lose herself in him before the night had even begun.

"Ava," Cal said as he stared into her hazel eyes so sensually.

With a lump in her throat, she barely let out, "Yes, Cal."

"What do you want?" Cal said in a low, seductive voice. "What are you hoping for tonight?"

Staring back at him, Ava took in his eyes, looking at her as if they knew exactly what she was thinking. "I…I'm not sure," Ava said with all sincerity. "I feel as if I've been transported back in time to high school," Ava said as she grabbed his hand that was resting on the center console. "You've always been able to make me feel wanted and special. I would be lying if I said I didn't feel the attraction too. But I can't help but think we are in the same place we were ten years ago. Living in two places didn't exactly work out for us last time. I don't want to hurt you again."

"Ava, I'm a big boy. I can take care of myself," Cal said, a little insulted.

"Okay, well then, I don't want a booty call either," Ava said, feeling defensive.

Cal, taken aback, said, "In what world are you ever a booty call? Ava, don't you know I respect you way too much to think of you like that? I mean, I thought we were headed toward marriage there for a while."

"You did?" Ava asked, surprised.

"Well, sure. To me there was no one else. And to be honest, there has never been anyone else," Cal said lowly.

Ava felt as though someone had just stabbed her with a knife through the heart. She knew if she were honest with herself that she had never truly felt the way she did about Cal with anyone else, including Eric.

"Cal...," Ava said as she trailed off. She didn't quite know how to respond. "From the bottom of my heart, I can't tell you how sorry I am that I was the one who broke us apart. Honestly, when you didn't come back for me or fight for our relationship, I thought it was the right decision."

"Wait a minute, when I didn't come back for you? What are you talking about, Ava?" Cal said, confused.

"After that day when we decided to break it off, you never came back or fought to keep the relationship, so I focused on my studies and tried to move on, but we can all see how well that went," Ava said as she rolled her eyes.

"Ava, you made it pretty clear that you would never move back to Iowa and that you did not want to be in a relationship with me, at least long distance. What was I supposed to do? Call you nonstop, drive up to your apartment every weekend, knowing it would just hurt you more? We were both a wreck after that day." Cal continued, "Honestly, I was hoping you would come back over summer break or something and we would find each other again. I guess I just thought it would have happened sooner."

"Well, I'm here now. A wreck with my personal life, but I'm here."

Cal took Ava's hand and said, "Well, then let's go enjoy this evening and start with one of your favorite dishes, unless that has changed too?"

Ava looked out the window and realized they were at Maverick's Surf and Turf, the fanciest restaurant in town, where they had dined on prom night.

"Oh, wow! Blast from the past! That sounds delicious," Ava said as they both hopped out of the truck.

As they entered the front doors, Ava was reminded of prom night all over again, as if it happened yesterday. They were two teenagers madly in love with the world at their fingertips.

In their best formal wear, they walked through the restaurant and sat at the table overlooking the lake, lit by candlelight.

That was the night Cal gave Ava a promise ring and pledged to love her forever.

The thought made Ava smile to think of how in love they once were.

"Ava, does this work for you?" Cal said, pointing to the table.

"Oh, sure!" Ava said and then realized it was the same table they had sat at ten years earlier.

Ava didn't want to say anything at first to Cal, but he was too quick and brought it up first. "I can't believe we came to prom here."

"I know it's hard to believe. It's been that long ago. But that was a fun night. So many good memories in this town," Ava said, trailing off and thinking of that night again.

The waiter approached the table, and Cal so elegantly ordered a bottle of Bubbly Moscato, confirming with Ava first if she still preferred a sweet white wine and the famous lemon butter garlic mussels.

Laughing out loud to herself, Ava said, "Are you trying to recreate that night?"

Cal chuckled. "Not necessarily. But I thought since we did enjoy them so much that night, we should give them another shot."

"Well, they were delicious," Ava said with a smile.

"And while on the topic of recreating that night, do you remember what I told you that evening?" Cal said as he reached his hand out across the table to grab Ava's hand.

"Remind me," Ava said, playing coy with a smirk on her face.

"I told you that I would love you forever, and I put this on your hand," Cal said as he pulled out a white gold ring with three small diamonds embedded in the band.

Ava's eyes grew wide. "Cal, what are you doing with this? I can't believe you kept this for so long."

"It's yours. You should have it. It's not like I would give it to someone else," Cal said as he placed the ring in the palm of her hand and enclosed Ava's fingers around the ring. "I told you that night that each diamond represented my love for you, which would never change. There was a diamond for yesterday, today, and tomorrow because my love would never fade. I would love you more than I did yesterday but not as much as I would tomorrow."

Remembering that night, Ava's eyes filled with tears. She tried to pull back her emotions, but it was no use.

Ava couldn't remember the last time she had someone be so genuine, romantic, and vulnerable.

"I do remember when you asked me to love you forever, Cal," Ava said, looking up at him with a single tear rolling down her cheek.

"It was the night I knew my heart would forever be yours."

Cal looked across the table at Ava and waited for the sign they had shared as a young couple—squeezing each other's hand three times to secretly tell each other, "I love you."

Just as Cal waited, the waiter arrived with the bottle of wine and appetizer.

Although they both thanked the waiter, neither one took their eyes off each other. Understanding the interruption, the waiter set the bottle and plate down. Then he quietly left.

Neither Cal nor Ava said anything for what seemed like an eternity. Ava's heart beat so fast she thought the entire restaurant could hear their unspoken conversation.

Rather than listen to reason, logic, or racing thoughts, Ava led with her heart for the first time in a while. She squeezed his hand—once, twice, and a third time.

Cal's look of wonder and doubt immediately changed to one of lust, wanting, and desire. He flagged down the waiter. "We'll take the check."

Ava felt a lump in her throat, wondering if she had done the right thing to let her emotions get the best of her, but it was too late to turn back now. She loved Cal and realized she always would.

She wondered how a man could hold on to something for so long, love someone for years, and still only want the best for them. It reminded her of her parents' love for each other.

The more Ava thought about how much she loved Cal, the more she wanted him.

16

Cal pushed his chair back and walked over to Ava's side of the table, bent down on one knee, and took Ava's hand in his.

Ava couldn't imagine what he was doing but was ready to take in the evening by following her heart.

Kissing Ava's hand gently and sliding on her old promise ring, Cal asked Ava to join him for an evening under the stars. Not understanding fully what Cal meant, Ava simply said yes.

Cal stood up and escorted Ava out the front entrance of Maverick's. Before they made it out the door, they were stopped by the owner asking if everything was okay with their dining experience.

"Oh, yes, Sam. Everything was just fine. There is an emergency that we need to attend to. We'll be back again soon," Cal said calmly but direct.

"Well, I hope everyone is okay," Sam said sincerely.

Ava's heart was pounding with excitement and the thrill of Cal's impromptu behavior. As he ushered Ava to his truck, she could hardly wait to see where they were going or what Cal had in mind for a night under the stars.

Regardless of what was planned, Ava knew she had never felt more like herself. She had never felt more alive than she did with Cal. He had a way of making her feel like she was the only one in the room.

As they approached the truck, Cal went to open Ava's door but instead twirled her around by the hand so she was facing him.

Eye to eye, they locked in on each other, and before Ava had a second to think about what could happen, Cal drew her into him and kissed Ava.

Cal brushed her hair off her face and pulled Ava in closer with his hands, caressing her body. Their kiss was soft and slow at first but grew to passion and longing.

Having not felt each other's touch in nearly ten years, they both yearned for each other more than they had each realized.

Ava matched his desire by grabbing on to his shirt and pulling him closer to her. She gradually moved her hands from clenching his shirt to running them through his thick dark hair.

Before too long, Cal had Ava pressed against his truck as they continued their ravenous kissing.

Cal pulled back to look at Ava, saying, "Where have you been?"

"Waiting..." Ava said breathlessly and aching for him not to stop.

"Oh, baby. If only I had known. I would have been there in a heartbeat," Cal said in a soft whisper.

Ava gazed at Cal, taking in his response. In that instant, Ava felt safe, emotionally and mentally. Something she longed for ever since they parted ways.

Lifting her lips to Cal, she gave him one more soft, sweet kiss before Ava pulled back and said in a low voice, "Cal, I need you."

Cal kissed Ava on the forehead and stepped back to open the passenger door. Confused that she said something too soon, Ava stepped backward and then got into the truck.

As Cal walked around to get in the driver's side, Ava leaned over to open the door for Cal.

Without saying one word, Cal started the truck, turned on the music, and headed off to show Ava the stars.

"Where are we going?" Ava asked, puzzled.

"Ava, I can't begin to tell you how long I've been waiting to hear you say those words to me. I've always needed you, but you never seemed like you needed me. Not really," Cal said.

Ava could tell that Cal was raw with emotions, and all she wanted was to hold him. She knew his pain was inflicted by her decision to break them apart.

Next thing Ava knew, the truck stopped. "We're here," Cal said.

Being nighttime, Ava couldn't make out all the intricate details, but she could see a large log cabin home on the edge of a lake that had a dock leading out to a boat.

"Wow, is this your home, Cal?" Ava said in amazement. "It's beautiful."

"It's a house. Still waiting for a family to make it a home," Cal said thoughtfully. "But it's where I lay my head at night," he said as he got out of the truck.

Ava opened her car door, and before she could hop out, Cal was right there to help her down.

Looking intently into her eyes, Ava thought Cal was going to surprise her with another kiss, but instead he grabbed her hand, closed the door behind her, and led her down a path toward the house.

Ava, excited to see the inside of Cal's home, was caught off guard when Cal bypassed the house and headed for the dock.

"Now, I promised a night under the stars," Cal said as they walked onto the pier.

"So I was thinking we could either sit here on the dock or if you wanted, we could take the boat out on the lake."

Realizing that Cal had grown into more than the boy she left behind, Ava decided to leave the evening up to Cal, saying, "Whichever you'd prefer sounds good to me."

"Let's take the boat." Cal gestured for her to step on board.

Cal and Ava took the boat out around the lake. There was a bit of a breeze, which helped keep them cool. After twenty minutes or so, Cal stopped the throttle and turned off the key in the ignition.

"It's funny. It's almost like we got a second chance, Ava," Cal said as he returned from casting the anchor.

There was no one else on the lake that night, but Cal knew the stars were most brilliant in the center, being farthest from any lights.

Cal went down to the galley and returned with a glass of rosé wine for Ava and a rocks glass of Tullamore Dew for himself.

Ava was surprised he had a wine she liked on the boat already. The idea that he had her drink of choice made her mind wonder if he had planned to take her there or if he often entertained other women on the boat.

"How did you know to have one of my favorites on board?" Ava said as she accepted the glass.

Cal smirked to himself. "Ava, I always have a stocked bar on the boat. Good host practice."

"Oh, I didn't know if it was because you entertained often on your boat or if you were expecting to bring me back here tonight," Ava said defensively.

"Well, I always hope to have more time with you, but no. I had no intentions for this evening other than having a nice evening with you," Cal said. He could see that Ava was still thinking about his answer.

"No, Ava, I do not bring other women here if that's what you're thinking. But if I did, would that bother you?"

Ava decided not to go down that path in her mind as she realized it caused her stomach to be in knots, thinking about Cal with another woman, even though they had not been together for a decade.

They sat next to each other on the bow, and Ava turned toward Cal, "A second chance, huh?" Ava paused for a moment to think about what that meant. "I like that idea—a second chance for us. But how will we avoid ending up in the same long-distance predicament we were in before?" Cal looked puzzled. Ava continued, "I mean, your work is here, and I wouldn't want you to give that up for anything. Your work is so impactful. And my work is in New York."

Ava look defeated and stressed. Cal moved his hand to massage her neck. "Ava, I'm not sure how it will all work out, but I do know that if we both want this, we will make it work. Do you want this, Ava? Do you want to be together again?" Cal said as he leaned in to hear her answer.

Ava was screaming the answer in her head but had trouble getting the words out of her mouth.

Cal stared at Ava, waiting for an answer that he had waited so long to hear again.

"I want you to be happy, Cal. I've always wanted that for you even if that's not with me. And if you're asking me to be part of that happiness, then my answer is yes!"

Wrapped up in emotion, Cal took Ava's face in both hands and kissed her ever so passionately.

The kiss was slow and sensual. The connection they once shared was still ignited between them, almost as though it had never left.

Cal scooped Ava up and moved her on top of him. She was consumed by him, taking each aspect in to remember the moment.

Ava began to unbutton Cal's oxford. Then, running her hands through his hair, she grabbed his neck as he picked her up, carrying Ava to the midcabin.

Laying her down gracefully on the dark-blue silk sheets, Cal stood back, taking off his shirt. As Ava's mind raced, she looked at him and still loved him as much as she ever had.

"Cal," Ava said as she pulled him toward her. "Make love to me. I need you."

17

As the sun rose over the mountains, the light danced across the lake, leaving sparkles in the water's wake. Ava awoke to the water lapping against the boat. So peacefully rested, she turned over to see if Cal was still there and it hadn't been a dream.

"Good morning, beautiful," Cal said as she turned toward him. "You seemed as if you were having a good dream, so I didn't want to wake you."

"Oh, really," Ava said, moving her hand across his face and down his chest. "I hope I didn't say anything too embarrassing."

Laughing, Cal said, "Nothing too damaging." He leaned in to kiss her, which led to another round of love making.

It was nearly 9:00 a.m. before Cal dropped Ava off back at her house. "That was an amazing night, Cal. Thank you for the stars," Ava said before she hopped out of the truck.

"Well, I should be done with my rounds tonight by eight. I know I took you away from your mom last night, but let me know if you would be up for dinner, drinks, or maybe a movie. You name it, and I'm there," Cal said happily.

"Ha, you're not sick of me yet," Ava said, laughing as she walked away.

Cal retorted quickly from his window as he began pulling away, "Aw, baby, that could never happen. Let me know about tonight. See you soon."

Ava waved goodbye and slowly began turning the handle when all of a sudden, the door flew open. "Ava!" Shelby shouted. "Is that you? Goodness, child. I thought you were in your room this whole time." Realizing that her daughter was just returning from her evening last night with Cal, she began smirking. "So just catching up with an old friend, huh?" Shelby said playfully.

"Oh, Mom," Ava said, not really wanting to talk about their entire evening or how they had obviously gotten closer than she had expected.

"Ava, I'm only going to say one thing," Shelby said, trying to be her mother but also her friend.

Thinking Shelby was going to lecture her, Ava rolled her eyes and turned toward her mom, about to justify her choices. After all she was an adult.

But what Shelby said next surprised Ava and made her realize that she might be a grown woman, but to her mom, she would always be her little girl.

"My hope for you has always been that you would be happy with yourself and then find a partner to walk through this life with that matches you in every way to make you whole. You are not responsible for making someone else happy, sweetheart. But to go through this life with a true partner by your side is the greatest gift that you could ever have." Ava began blushing as Shelby continued on, "I see the way Cal looks at you. The man cannot hide the way he feels about you. He never could."

"You think so?" Ava said obtusely.

Shelby, knowing her daughter's statement was foolish, said, "Oh, please. You were just as obvious about him as he was about you. Ava, you two are a match made in heaven. From the day you brought him home, your dad and I knew. We knew we were in trouble."

They both laughed, remembering the day Ava introduced Cal to her parents.

Shelby grabbed Ava's hands and patted them gently. Then she raised her head to meet Ava's eyes. "Sweetie, just follow your heart, and you will never have any regrets."

Letting Shelby's last statement sink in, Ava thought that those were powerful words. A world without any regrets sounded blissful to Ava.

"Well now, what shall we do today?" Shelby asked Ava. "Do you have to work today, or are we free to do girl stuff? I do have a doctor's appointment today, but other than that, I am free."

"Oh, well, I was going to work for the morning, but then I could be open. But I do want to go with you to your appointment. What time is it?" Ava asked.

"It's right before lunch at 11:00 a.m."

"Perfect. I'll work for a little bit, get ready, and then I can drive you there. Are you up for grabbing lunch out after your appointment?" Ava asked, uplifted that Shelby felt well enough to be out on the town.

"That sounds lovely, dear. Okay, I will be ready to head out at ten forty-five," Shelby said, confirming their departure time.

Ava decided to quickly get ready so she could work until the last minute before leaving for the doctor's appointment.

As she sat down to focus in on work, she realized that she had received confirmation from both parties regarding the merger.

The final word was in, and they both accepted the terms and conditions. All the pieces were falling into place, and Ava was one step closer to not having to work for Jackie anymore.

Ava quickly responded to both Addison and Parker and Stokes with the affirmative that all addenda and original terms of the contracts had been accepted.

The final paperwork would be drawn up within the week for both companies to sign, and at the end of the quarter, which happened to be in a few weeks, they would officially become Parker, Stokes, Addison, and Associates.

Ava sent another e-mail to her management team and the merger team, cc'ing Jackie, stating the merger was 99 percent complete.

Once the final addenda were put into place and finalized by their legal department, we would have one of the largest mergers Truman Partners had seen to date.

After notifying management of this big win, Ava sent an e-mail to Silvia, asking if, once the signed paperwork was returned by carrier, she could please send over welcome baskets to both Parker and Stokes as well as Addison, congratulating them on bringing two amazing companies together under one roof.

Finally, her last e-mail was to HR and Jackie. Ava explained that Shelby was doing better with her recovery, but that she would be staying at least one more week until the doctor released her from needing in-home assistance.

As Ava wrapped up her last e-mail, she heard Shelby shouting, "Ava, come on! Let's go, please. I don't want to be late."

Ava powered down her laptop, grabbed her purse, and headed toward the living room.

18

Ava and Shelby entered the doctor's office to find that they would be seeing Dr. Sophie today as Dr. Michael's was on call at the hospital today.

Remembering that Cal said he would be on rounds until later that night, she understood why she wouldn't see Cal at the visit but found herself disappointed that she wasn't going to see him until later.

Dr. Sophie was pleased overall with Shelby's recovery and numbers. She mentioned that typically, with a minor stroke, the recovery time could be anywhere from a few months to a year.

The fact that Shelby was mobile and mentally aware gave Dr. Sophie confidence that in another week, she would be in the clear for any permanent damage from the stroke.

Ava was still concerned that Shelby could relapse; however, Dr. Sophie reminded her that since Shelby was not experiencing weakness or numbness that this was a strong sign of a full recovery.

Dr. Sophie did remind Shelby to continue to take it slow. Although her mind seemed to be recovering well, that didn't mean her body didn't need more time to recuperate.

Ava and Shelby thanked Dr. Sophie for her time and headed to check out with Caroline.

"Caroline, how are you?" Ava said as if she was catching up with one of her friends.

"I'm well, dear. Thank you," Caroline said. Looking at Shelby, her voice and demeanor changed, "Shell, are you okay? You look faint."

Before Caroline could finish her sentence, Shelby went weak in the knees and fell to the floor.

"Mom!" Ava screamed.

Caroline immediately picked up the phone, and Ava could hear her bark out a code, which she could only assume meant medical attention was required immediately.

Before Ava could understand what was going on, three nurses surrounded Shelby, and Dr. Sophie was on the phone telling the hospital to prep for the arrival of Shelby Stillman.

Not having been around when Shelby was taken to the Meadow Brook Hospital the first time, the severity of the situation became ever so real for Ava.

Riding in the ambulance with Shelby, Ava grabbed her hand and kept repeating, "Mom, just hang in there. We'll be there soon. Stay with me."

Arriving to the hospital, the paramedics jumped out of the front and were at the back doors within seconds.

Medical staff swarmed the ambulance, and Ava saw Cal rushing to meet them.

"Dr. Sophie called it in. Where do we stand?" Cal demanded.

As if routine, the paramedics told Cal Shelby's stats and that she had yet to wake from when she fainted at Dr. Griffin's offices.

Ava intended to follow everyone, but when they approached the doors, she was met by Gracie who led her to the waiting area for ICU patients.

"Ava, its Gracie. Remember me? Let me show you to the waiting area, and as soon as we know more about Shelby's condition, I will come right out and tell you," Gracie said in a calming voice.

Although Ava understood everything that Gracie was saying, she was in shock from the morning's ordeal.

She simply followed Gracie and sat down to wait.

A few hours later, Gracie came out to find Ava, who was anxiously waiting. "Ava." Gracie beckoned. "Would you like to see your mom?"

"Yes, thank you, Gracie. Is she okay? What happened?"

"Ava, Shelby is stable, but let the doctors explain." Not knowing much in the medical field, Ava didn't think that this was good news.

As Ava approached Shelby's room, she entered cautiously. To her surprise, Shelby was awake and talking with Cal and Dr. Sophie.

"Mom!" Ava yelled as she ran over to her bedside and embraced her in a hug that seemed to last forever. "Mom, I was so worried. I didn't know what to think. Thank goodness we were at the doctor's office when this happened. Not sure I would have known what to do if we were by ourselves."

"I hope you would have done just what we did today. Brought her to the hospital to get tested and checked," said Dr. Sophie.

"So I don't understand. Why does this keep happening? Is she going to be okay?" Ava asked in a panicked attempt to get answers.

"Ava, we now believe Shelby did not suffer a minor stroke but rather some of her internal organs are shutting down, and we need to understand the cause to treat it properly. This is why after she was treated here last time, her body was able to maintain the status quo for a few weeks. Then, as Shelby began exerting more energy, trying to get back to her normal day-to-day, her body gave out again," said Dr. Sophie.

"I don't understand what that means. Are you saying that she is restricted to her house? And if she does anything strenuous that she will end up in the hospital?" Ava said.

"Ava, right now your mom's heart is working overtime trying to help her other organs function as they should. A few weeks ago when she was in here, she slipped into a coma-like state where her body was resting to rejuvenate from the medicine we were giving her. Now, we are essentially right back to where we started two weeks ago. However this time, we know to look more closely at some numbers that before we attributed to what we thought was a stroke."

Cal continued on, trying to calm Ava, "So now, we need to find the right mixture of medicine to help balance Shelby's kidneys so they can process as they should. This will allow her other organs, like her heart, to not be overworked and hopefully, return to normal function, if we can hone in on the right combination of meds."

Trying to comprehend what was being explained to her, Ava asked, "Okay, so if we find the right combination, then she will feel better? And return to life before this craziness started?"

"Yes, that is the idea."

Cal and Dr. Sophie excused themselves so they could go review the latest labs and discuss a plan of action for prescribing the right medicine for Shelby.

"I'm sorry that you had to see all this, Ava. But I'm glad you were with me this time. It's a little scary when this happens and I come to," Shelby commented.

"I can only imagine, Mom. But I'm right here, and I'm not going anywhere until we get you healthy."

"That's sweet of you, but I don't want to be a bother, and I don't want you missing more work because of me," Shelby said, concerned.

"Mom, everything happens for a reason, and family comes first," Ava said with assertiveness. "If my company can't understand that, then that is just one more reason not to work for them."

"Well, since it turns out I did not have a stroke, promise me once they figure out the medicine issue, that you will go back and put your work issues to rest. You need to be at peace with this so you can be happy, sweetheart. I know you love what you do, Ava, and I don't want any man to stand in the way of your dreams."

"Mom, maybe dreams are meant to be changed," Ava said excitedly.

Right as Ava was going to tell Shelby about Cal and her making a go of them as a couple, they heard a rapping at the door. They both glanced over and saw Eric standing there with a bouquet of flowers.

Ava was in shock and could immediately feel her blood begin to boil, but she wanted to keep her emotions composed as to not rile up Shelby. But before Ava could get two words out, Shelby took the lead.

"Eric!" Shelby announced.

"Hello, Mrs. Stillman. I'm glad to see that you are feeling better," Eric said as quietly as a church mouse.

Ava couldn't determine what his end goal was. Did he want to come and prove he was innocent in everything or was he checking up on Shelby because he thought that would make Ava forgive him?

Ava, still not saying anything to Eric, stood up from Shelby's bedside.

Surprising Ava, Shelby continued to speak to Eric, "How nice of you to come and see us. Especially after you cheated on my daughter and she caught you in the act. Now, I'm not sure how you were raised, young man, but I didn't realize men in New York were under the impression that an apology could fix screwing around on someone you supposedly love. No self-respecting man treats a woman that way. Shame on you."

Eric stood dumbfounded, and Ava couldn't believe that Shelby managed to strip him down emotionally without raising her temperament.

There was always something to be said about a mother protecting her child, even if she couldn't get out of the hospital bed to smack him upside the head.

"Eric, let's step outside and talk," Ava said curtly.

Ava led Eric to the garden, which was directly outside Shelby's room.

"Ava, I am so sorry. Please forgive me," Eric said with his hands folded, pleading with Ava.

"Jackie didn't mean anything to me. I swear this will never happen again. I love you. I want to marry you. Please come back to me, baby. I miss you so much. This was a huge mistake. I should have never gotten involved with Jackie. Please forgive me and come back to New York."

Ava let him ramble on, and then when he finished talking, she said, "Are you done?"

As Eric started to speak again, Ava raised her hand to stop him and said, "That was more rhetorical. I honestly have nothing to say to you, nor do I care to hear anything you have to say. You are an asshole who only cares about himself. I am done with you and whatever we were to each other. I do not care to see you ever."

Surprised by Ava's response, Eric stumbled backward and could see that Ava had somehow become stronger in the weeks since she left.

"I am sorry I hurt you, Ava. I did and still do love you. Please don't hate me. We can make this work."

Eric continued to plead for Ava to forgive him, but Ava simply did not care to hear anything that he had to say.

For the first time in a long time, Ava was happy with herself and with a man who made her feel loved, respected, and cherished.

"Eric, I don't hate you because the only person who suffers in that scenario is me. I don't care to spend one more ounce of my time thinking about you or what you did. I simply don't care."

Ava extended her hand and asked for her apartment key back.

As she did this, Cal saw from Shelby's room that Ava was talking with a man, who Shelby then explained was Eric.

Cal immediately wanted to walk out to the garden and pulverize Eric for hurting Ava the way he did, but then he saw Ava extend her hand to Eric, and he reciprocated.

Cal, heavyhearted and hurt, looked away from them. He assumed Ava had forgiven Eric and that the other night meant nothing to her.

Discouraged by what he saw, Cal delivered the news he intended to when he walked into Shelby's room.

Cal believed he and the team identified what was causing her kidneys to fail. They were going to start her on a new cocktail of medicine to make her feel better and keep her for a few more days of observation to ensure their findings were correct.

Not understanding the change in Cal's tone, Shelby asked, "Cal, are you okay? You seem distracted."

Cal looked straight out the window at Ava and Eric. "No, Shelby. Everything is just fine. We will get you back to feeling good in no time." Then he walked out of Shelby's room.

Confused by his change in demeanor, Shelby looked out her window at the garden where she saw Ava standing proud with her head held high.

She turned and walked back toward the hospital doors, and Shelby watched as Eric gazed at Ava as she walked away.

Eric threw up his hands and ran them down the back of his head. She could tell he felt defeated and knew he just lost the best thing that happened to him. He then turned around and walked out toward the parking lot.

Not worthy of my daughter, you pathetic excuse for a man, Shelby thought to herself as Dr. Sophie walked into her room.

"Shelby, are you feeling okay? Your blood pressure is sky high. Your other vitals look good though. Is something bothering you?" Dr. Sophie asked concerned as she gauged Shelby's vital signs.

"Oh, I'm doing great. I just watched my daughter stand up for herself and walk away with her head held high. A mother can't ask for anything better," Shelby said with a big smile on her face.

Dr. Sophie smiled. "Yes, I suppose you are correct. Well, Dr. Michaels said that he relayed the news about the new mix of meds that we're going to try, and if all goes as planned, we should have you out of here in a few days."

Hearing the tail end of the conversation, Ava said, "Oh, Mom, that's great news! This day just keeps getting better and better."

"Well, we still have to monitor, but we think with the new labs we ran, this will help the underlying condition, which should then relieve the dizziness and weakness that keep occurring," Dr. Sophie said.

They all seemed uplifted by the good news, and Dr. Sophie left them to return to the doctor's offices.

It was late afternoon. After Shelby finished eating, she had fallen asleep. Ava thought it would be a good opportunity to find Cal.

Ava headed down the hall toward the nurses' station to ask for Dr. Michaels, but as she approached, she saw Cal at the end, writing in a patient's chart.

Walking over to where Cal stood, Ava playfully said, "Hi there."

"Hi, Ava, is Shelby doing okay?" Cal said coldly.

"Yes, she is asleep right now, so I thought I would come find you and see if you're available for a lovely cafeteria dinner," Ava said, chuckling.

Cal picked up the chart he was writing in and looked at Ava before he walked away, saying, "Ava, getting over you was the most difficult thing I've ever had to do, and I don't want to do it again. I wish nothing but the best for you, and I hope you find happiness. But I can't do this back-and-forth, waiting to see what comes of it."

Shocked and feeling her heart come to a slow beat, Ava was confused and speechless.

As Cal walked away, Ava tried to recall what happened from last night that would make him change his mind. *He seemed convinced last night that we could make it work if that was what we both wanted.*

Not understanding why Cal changed his mind, Ava's heart hurt again from the sting of letting Cal go. She wanted nothing more than to be with him again. But he wasn't willing to work it out, and Ava had to deal with his decision.

Walking into Shelby's room, Ava quietly sat down on the chair next to her mother's bed. Ava looked out the window at the garden silently as a single tear rolled down her face.

Thinking about the wonderful evening she had with Cal last night and the love they made only caused Ava to be more upset about what could have been.

Once again, Ava pushed the idea of having a family out of her mind, and she focused on what would happen with her career.

Ava pondered all the scenarios that could occur now that she no longer wanted to work with Jackie at Truman Partners. She figured another firm was always an option, but if she was starting over, did she really want to live in New York?

A dream of Ava's was to always reach the C level of an organization to really make an impact and difference for not only the company but the people that worked for the company.

She knew her perspective would be an asset to any executive team if they would just allow her to utilize her leadership skill set.

Gracie was on duty that evening at the hospital. "Hello, Ava," Gracie said as she entered Shelby's room. "Hi, Gracie, how are you doing?" Ava said, happy to see a friendly face.

"I should be asking you the same question. It must have been an emotional roller coaster today with all this. But it sounds like we're on the right track with the new meds," Gracie said.

"Yes, it certainly does," Ava said as she stared at Shelby sleeping.

"Well, in a day or so, we will run the tests again. Then if all the numbers come back good, she should be all set to go home," Gracie said, hopeful. "I sure hope she gets better soon. We miss having her here volunteering with us."

"I'm sure she misses it too. Mom has always enjoyed taking care of others," Ava said, admiring that attribute about Shelby.

"Well, I will let you two get some sleep," Gracie said as she left the room and turned down the lights.

19

Three days had passed, and Ava was at Shelby's house, finishing up work e-mails before heading to pick up Shelby from the hospital.

The blood work came back, and Shelby's kidneys were now filtering out the toxins from the blood and excreting them.

Dr. Sophie was very detailed when she gave Ava the paperwork about how to best prepare the house for Shelby's return home.

She told Ava that hydration was key to balance the body, but cranberry juice, apples, oatmeal, and mushrooms were wonderful for the kidneys. So Ava stocked the house with these groceries.

On the sheet Ava had from Dr. Sophie were other healthy reminders, such as eat healthy and exercise regularly, which Shelby already did. But Ava created loving sticky notes with these reminders and placed them all over the house.

Ava was beyond relieved that Shelby was coming home today as Ava finally had all the paperwork for the Parker, Stokes,

Addison, and Associates merger complete. She had a few hours of conference calls with both sides yesterday and solidified all the dates and details of the addendum.

Following their signing yesterday, Ava had decided to return to New York and put in her resignation to Truman Partners before she was put on another merger project.

Ava had scheduled a meeting with the head of human resources next Monday, where she planned to hand in her resignation in person, give two weeks' notice, and thank the executive team in person for all they had done for her over the past ten years.

The idea that Ava would no longer work for Truman Partners was bittersweet. She loved working for the firm, but Ava knew to work alongside Jackie was not an option for her.

When Ava picked Shelby up from the hospital, she was dressed and ready to go before Ava walked in the room.

"Wow, Mom. One would think you were excited to head home," Ava said, laughing.

"Oh, honey, yes I am. I can't wait to sleep in my own bed, cook my own meals, and be back in my own home," Shelby said excitedly.

"Well, good because I have prepared it with all sorts of yummy foods," Ava said.

"Sweetheart, I could have gone grocery shopping. I can take care of myself, you know," Shelby said with a smile.

Ava retorted, "Yes, I know, Mom, but I wanted to make sure you had everything you needed before I left for New York in a few days."

"I'll be fine. Plus, with you visiting more often, I have more to look forward to," Shelby said as she grabbed her purse, and they walked out of the hospital room.

"Yes, I promise. I will be back in a few weeks to visit again. Just as soon as—"

Right as Shelby and Ava turned out of the room, they ran into Cal, which stopped Ava from speaking.

"Hi, Shelby, glad to see you are heading home today."

"Ava, hello, heading back to New York soon?" Cal asked.

Cal's question stung more than Ava thought. "Yes, in a few days."

"Well, have a safe flight," Cal said as he walked away.

Shelby and Ava continued walking toward the parking lot. Confused by Cal's shortness, Shelby asked, "What was that about? Did you two have words?"

"No, no, Mom. Nothing like that. No need to worry. Cal and I are still best of friends," Ava said, not believing her own words.

"Friends," Shelby said, getting into the passenger side of the car. "I thought the other night was more than just friends hanging out. What did I miss when I was in the hospital?"

"Honestly, I don't know. We were thick as thieves, just like the old days, but then something changed. Maybe he got spooked. Don't worry, Mom. I'm fine," Ava said again, as though repeating herself would make it true.

They continued their small talk all the way home and did not speak about Cal again.

In a few days, Shelby felt well enough that Ava decided to head back to New York. She made Shelby promise to call her if anything was wrong or she didn't feel well. Ava promised to come home as soon as she got the call.

Shelby's heart felt heavy as she watched her daughter leave for the airport. Although she had come home under poor circumstances, Shelby thoroughly enjoyed having her daughter home.

Ava waved to Shelby from the taxi window and realized how much she missed being home around her mom. She vowed in that moment that she would make it home once a month no matter what her work schedule was.

The flight back to New York was long but somewhat peaceful as Ava had already made the decision to resign from Truman Partners. Ava still had knots in her stomach from how things ended with Cal.

She wished they would have ended up together as they were meant to be. *But everything happened for a reason,* she thought.

As Ava opened the door to her apartment, she looked around, and the home that once felt love and full of life was now filled with emptiness.

Having been at her childhood home for a few months had reminded Ava of what she wanted to come home to each night.

In that moment, Ava knew she did not want to stay in New York. No matter where she looked, it reminded her of a life she once had and one she no longer wanted.

Over the weekend, Ava prepared her letter of resignation to give to Carol-Ann. Initially, Ava thought she would feel nervous or wonder if she was making the right decision, but Ava was strangely calm.

She knew it was the right decision for her and her sanity.

By Monday morning, Ava walked into the office and was greeted with a warm hug from Silvia. *This was unusual for the office environment in the big city,* Ava thought to herself.

"Silvia, wow, thank you for the warm greeting." Ava laughed. "Is everything okay?"

Silvia composed herself. "Oh, yes, Ms. Stillman. We just all heard the news, and my heart went out to you."

For a minute, Ava thought that Silvia might be talking about the affair between Jackie and Eric, but then Silvia said, "I just can't imagine how nerve-racking the whole ordeal was with your mother. But thank goodness she is doing better. And we are so thankful to have you back!"

"Oh, Mrs. Beck, well, thank you for your kind words. I very much appreciate the welcome sentiment after being away for so long. It's a comfort for sure," Ava said as she thought about her small hometown.

Ava walked down the hall to her corner office and got settled into her desk. She spun her chair around and took a long, hard look out the window at her office view and thought to herself for a split second, *Am I ready to give all this up? Yes!*

Nine o'clock rolled around quicker than she had expected, but Ava stood with her head held high and marched into her meeting with Carol-Ann.

"Ava, welcome back. Please come in," Carol-Ann said as she waved her hand to one of the chairs.

"Thank you, Carol-Ann, for making the time to see me so early on a Monday. I know the executive team has their staff meetings at ten, so I won't take too much of your time," Ava said with her voice strong and not shaking.

"Ava, you're always welcome to come see me. We were very concerned about your mother's condition, but that's great news that she is doing better. All of us were very impressed that among the difficulty of dealing with a personal, family matter, you were still able to close the deal with Parker, Stokes, and Addison. You truly are amazing at what you do, Ava. And Truman Partners is lucky to have you on our team."

Ava felt a lump in her throat but told herself to remember why this couldn't continue and what she had to do for her self-worth.

"Carol-Ann, thanks for your kindness and the company allowing me to work remote for a few months while I took care of my mother. I will never forget that this was extended to me as well as the team recognizing my diligent efforts to conclude the merger."

Ava looked down at her letter of resignation and with a bit of pause, handed it across the desk to Carol-Ann. She felt as though she was forfeiting the last ten years of her life, but she knew it was the right thing to do.

Carol-Ann read the letter and looked up at Ava, stunned. "Ava, I'm a little surprised. Is it your mother? Is she not doing better? We can certainly work with you if you need more time with her."

"While I appreciate that, Carol-Ann, it's become a different matter as to why I need to leave," Ava said firmly.

"Need to leave? Is there something I can do to have you stay with us? We do not want to lose you, Ava. You are critical to our team. I can talk to management, and we can look to include an increase in pay and perhaps remoting every so often so you can visit your mom."

"Wow, Carol-Ann, that is an incredible offer, but I simply cannot continue to work with Jackie. It's a personal matter of conflicting ethics, and I have reached my threshold of what I will condone. It has absolutely nothing to do with Truman Partners. I love this company. It's where I got my start and big wins, both personally and professionally."

Taken aback, Carol-Ann leaned backward in her chair. "Well, I cannot make you stay. Although I wish you'd reconsider. I do understand that if it's a matter of personal issue, that's something that is not going to rectify itself overnight. And gauging from your disposition, I can see that you have weighed this decision heavily."

"Yes, I have. I am sorry that I will not be able to continue with Truman Partners. It has been my second home," Ava said candidly.

"Ava, please know that you always have a place here at Truman Partners."

"Thank you, Carol-Ann. I greatly appreciate that, and I just may take you up on that should circumstances change," Ava said.

"Thank you for doing this in person, Ava. And we will send a notice out to all staff, letting them know of your departure," Carol-Ann said.

"Now, I will share this in our executive meeting this morning, so you may receive some calls from management today."

"Understood. Thanks for the heads up," Ava said with a small smile on her face as she stood up from the chair.

Ava walked back to her office with a sense of pride that she stood up for herself, even if it meant giving up a job she loved.

Since the merger with Parker, Stokes, and Addison had completed, Ava wanted to notify them that she would only be around another two weeks to answer any questions or tie up loose ends should they have any, so she sent an e-mail.

Hi, Parker, Stokes, and Addison,

Welcome to the family! As my first official e-mail to the leaders of the newly organized company, I wanted to send along my personal congratulations and hope the employees of both organizations are as excited as you three are to have the marriage official.

I also wanted to notify the team that I gave my notice today, and as of next Friday,

Sally Reider will be your new contact at Truman Partners, should you have any questions. As the time gets closer, I will send along an introduction e-mail so everyone has each other's contact information.

This is a bittersweet parting, but I am looking forward to my new adventure. If you should need anything in the interim, please feel free to reach out.

Thank you again for your trust, time, and patience with me as we worked through this merger to make it as successful for all parties as possible.

Thank you,
Ava Stillman
VP of Strategic Partnerships
Truman Partners

Just as Ava finished hitting send, she looked up to find Jackie leaning in her doorway with her arms crossed in front of her.

Ava's face felt flush, and her sense of betrayal was ripe with emotion. Even though she had no feelings toward Eric, she still could not wrap her head around how Jackie could be so treacherous.

"Hello, Ava. Welcome back!" Jackie said as though nothing had happened.

Ava looked back down at her e-mails and worked very hard at keeping her cool although her response came out icier than anticipated. "Thank you."

Trying to continue a conversation in the workplace, Jackie said, "I saw that the Parkers, Stokes, and Addison deal came through. Great work. While you were out, I covered for you on another merger that's coming in, but now that you have returned, I'll begin to forward everything over so you can get caught up. Then I'll make the intro call with you and the clients."

Ava began to respond, but behind Jackie came Carol-Ann's voice. "Oh, Jackie, great. I was just looking for you. I don't think you'll need to transfer anything to Ava as she submitted her resignation this morning."

Jackie's jaw dropped and stammered, "Oh, oh. I guess Ava and I hadn't had a chance to catch up on that yet."

"Well, no concerns there. However, management and I would like to have a conversation with you. Now if you're available," Carol-Ann said in a strict tone that really wasn't asking if she was free but more telling her that she would be going with her.

"Oh, certainly. Now works fine," Jackie said to Carol-Ann as she looked at Ava, trying to read her face to see what Ava disclosed to HR.

Carol-Ann turned to Ava and said, "Ava, we had our executive meeting this morning, and if you could head upstairs to the E suite, the team would like to meet with you before lunch today, if possible."

"Sure thing, Carol-Ann. I'll head up there momentarily. Thanks," Ava said with a sense of satisfaction.

When Ava got home that evening, she replayed the meetings with the President, Executive Presidents, and chiefs of the company.

They were very interested in hearing Ava's plans, and several offered to have her return, should her plans change. All the teammates offered Ava a great sense of gratitude for her tenure and years of service to the company.

They reiterated what Carol-Ann had said about being an asset and that she would be missed.

Everything Ava heard made her sad to leave the company but amazed at the same time to know that her work was not only recognized but appreciated by all levels in the company.

Ava called Shelby that night and told her how it went with the resignation and the meeting with Jackie in her doorway but how it was interrupted by HR. Shelby laughed at the thought of karma.

"So what's next, dear?" Shelby asked Ava inquisitively.

"I'm not sure, Mom. But I have a few feelers out there now with headhunters and some contacts. I know something will come through, but I simply couldn't work there another day with Jackie," Ava said matter-of-factly.

Just then, Ava received another call. "Mom, I have a work call coming in. I'll call you tomorrow, okay? Glad you're feeling well. Love you."

As Ava hung up the phone with her mom, she half thought of letting it go to voice mail.

"Ava Stillman," she answered assertively.

"Ava, Mark Addison. Sorry to call you after-hours, but I wanted to discuss something with you. Do you have a few minutes?" Mark asked in a friendly manner.

Not exactly sure what Mark could want as the deal had finished, quite successfully from Ava's perspective. "Hi, Mr. Addison, certainly. How can I be of assistance?"

"Ava, for the hundredth time, please call me Mark," he said with a smile.

A little disturbed that Addison was calling after-hours to make niceties, Ava responded a little sterner that she had intended, "How can be of assistance, Mark?"

"Well, I was speaking with Parker and Stokes, and we were very impressed, as we all had mentioned on numerous occasions, with how you handled our merger. And we were surprised to hear of your departure from Truman Partners."

"Yes, I know it does seem sudden, but there was a change that occurred that needed my attention. But I promise you, the team is still in excellent hands," Ava said, knowing her soon to be former company would take exceptional care of them through the transition.

"I'm sure you already have something lined up, but we were hoping we might be able to sway you to come and work for us!" Mark said enthusiastically.

A bit speechless, Ava responded, "Wow, Mark, I'm not sure what to say here."

"Maybe don't say anything just yet. Let me share our proposal with you, and then you can think about it and get back to us in two weeks," Mark said confidently.

And as if Ava had agreed to the terms already, Mark continued on his soapbox.

"Parker, Stokes, and I spoke about this in great length, but we all came to the same conclusion. We need you to be on our team to help guide us toward a successful path and lead our team to the potential you saw when you positioned our companies together. I know this is a big ask, Ava, but we are willing to make you an offer, hopefully, you cannot refuse."

Ava was in utter shock at the quick turn of events. She wondered how this would all shape out and if it were a conflict of interest since they were clients of Truman Partners.

If she were to seriously consider this, Ava would need to go back and review the terms of her employee agreement in the noncompete clause.

"Mark, I am not sure what to say exactly. I am honored that the team holds me in such high regard and believes in my leadership to want me on your team," Ava said, flattered.

"So say I was to be interested in joining Parker, Stokes, Addison, and Associates. How do you envision me applying my contract negotiations and company merger talents to work for your firm? And along the same vein, let's also talk logistics. Parker and Stokes are headquartered out of Manhattan, and you are in St. Louis."

Mark had a deep, hearty laugh. "Oh, Ava, you never cease to amaze me. Your mind is always working overtime it seems." He continued, "Yes, first, logistics. As we see it, you did such a great job for us, even when you had a personal situation, that you gave us the confidence that you can do your work virtually anywhere. We would probably want you on-site, perhaps between the two locations, for a few weeks. But then you can choose which site suits you best. Then if you need to be with your family to take care of your mother, we can look to a remote position, where you visit each location quarterly."

Ava was taken aback that they had put so much thought into this without a response in the affirmative yet.

"The way we see it, Ava, we know your talents are an extreme asset, and as our motto in doing this merger stood, our employees come first. Understanding your people and what drives them is a good indicator of great leadership. We recognized that your family came first, but in all the chaos, you still came through for us. We recognize that and appreciate your efforts. As such, we would like to invite you to be a part of our team as the new EVP of Strategic Partnerships and Efficiency."

Ava thought about how fancy of a title that seemed but didn't necessarily understand how this would play into their newly formed company. "Mark, how do you see this role unfolding as the company matures?"

"I'm so glad you asked, Ava. You're always thinking a few steps ahead! Well, after the dust settles—if you will, in a few weeks—we would like for you to initially complete your walk-through of evaluating partnerships, overlap, and make suggestions for growth. It is during this time that we would like you to meet with the employees of the company. Once this is underway with your direction, we see this being handed off to our HR department to complete. Then we would like to apply your talents in undertaking an assessment of our combined companies, negotiating out the best scenarios for maximum efficiencies, and advising us on next steps. From there, we were thinking of continual evaluation of our systems, platforms, contract negotiations for newer tools and resources in the industry for us to capitalize on, new markets to get involved with, and selectively choosing how to lead the way in our market."

Absorbing all the new information, Ava's mind raced with so many questions and wondered if leaving the corporate world with the high-rise office where she worked daily on big mergers and acquisitions was what she wanted to leave.

Surely, she would find another job where she would have a similar scope of work as at Truman Partners, but was that what she wanted?

Ava considered Mark's offer before responding, "Mark, what you have laid out sounds like a remarkable opportunity, and I can see how my efforts would be a symbiotic relationship. However—"

"Ava, before you say anything or give us an answer, please take a few weeks to consider. As far as pay and benefits are concerned, we would like to offer you a role on our executive team, which means that all health and insurance benefits would be at no cost to you. Additionally, we would like to offer you a salary of $150,000, which we know probably does not compete with what you are making now. However, in addition to this base pay, we would also like to extend a 3 percent annual earning bonus from our year-end total profits."

Since Ava had run their numbers for the agreement, she knew independently each company profited net in excess of a million annually.

Thus, if they were able to get their overhead cost down as she had recommended in her analysis of the merged portfolios, this could be even more sizable.

"Since you are helping to shape this company, we feel it is only right that you see a bit of the action. So Parker, Stokes, and I are each giving you 1 percent of our annual profit earnings. This is of course separate from any bonuses and performance increases."

"Mark, this is an extremely generous offer," Ava said in all sincerity.

"We are very serious about having you join our team and are willing to make a fair and reasonable offer to get you on board. Now, as I mentioned, please don't give us an answer today. Really take the time to finish everything at Truman and close one chapter. We realize it is a shift from what you are currently doing, and we can see that you love what you do," Mark said genuinely.

"Well, please extend my sincere thanks to the rest of the team for thinking of me for such a role. I will consider it and give you my answer before the end of the month," Ava said, looking at the calendar.

"Thank you, Ava. We appreciate you considering us, and if you decide to join the team, I will have the paperwork drawn up and sent over to you," Mark said hopefully. "Have a good evening, Ava."

"You as well, Mark."

20

Two weeks had passed, and Ava had wrapped everything up at Truman Partners. She couldn't believe that time had gone by so quickly. It would be difficult to say goodbye to a life she had known for nearly a decade.

She made her rounds with the executive team, saying goodbye. Many of whom wished her well in her next venture and reminded her that she would always have a place at Truman Partners.

As Ava made her way to Silvia's desk, she took out the gift she had bought for her—a gold pendant with diamonds and pearls. "Mrs. Beck, how are you doing this fine Friday?" Ava said, smiling from ear to ear.

"Oh, Ava, I will miss you so much. I can't believe you are really leaving. I surely thought that I would be retiring before you even considered leaving Truman. You will certainly be missed," Silvia said with a genuine tone as she looked down at her desk, trying to find something to concentrate on rather than Ava.

"Well, Mrs. Beck, you have certainly been a good friend to me while I was here and as such, I got you a little something," Ava said as she reached into her suit jacket pocket and pulled out a small jewelry box.

Ava handed the box over to Silvia. With a moment of disbelief, Silvia extended her hand to take the box. She loosened the golden ribbon and opened the crimson-colored box to reveal the pendant studded with diamonds and pearls.

With nearly tears in her eyes, Silvia simply looked up from behind her desk and said, "Thank you, Ms. Stillman."

Ava, with an enormous smile, said, "Mrs. Beck, you are so welcome. Thank you for always taking the time to talk with me on our elevator rides for more coffee and offering to be of assistance with any project. I, too, will miss working with you. And please, call me Ava."

Silvia, overcome with emotion, stood up, came around her desk, and embraced Ava in a hug. Silvia said to Ava, "You are an incredible person both inside and out. Any organization is lucky to have you. If you ever need anything, please don't be a stranger."

"I won't, Mrs. Beck. Have a wonderful weekend, and we will certainly keep in touch," Ava said as she walked back toward her office to pack her remaining items.

As Ava turned the corner, heading to her office, she passed Jackie's office or what use to be her office. The company had recognized that Jackie's lack of leadership and ethical conundrums extended to others in the organization as well, which led to her demotion.

Jackie now resided on the second floor with other managers who oversaw internal projects, rather than dealing with client-facing relations.

Although Ava didn't think Jackie would stay in that position very long, she did have an inward tingle as she passed by her office, knowing that her true colors had shone through for the higher-ups to see, and they took action.

Ava was packing up her office when she heard a ding from her personal e-mail on her phone. She glanced over to read her inbox.

Greetings Ava,

Hope all is going well on your last day at Truman Partners. We thank you for bringing to our attention about your noncompete clause and the circumstances that surround the agreement.

We appreciate your due diligence and ethical consideration in taking our offer to your HR department to see what possibilities exist between us hiring you, considering we were a client of Truman Partners.

I guess all the stars aligned that you had submitted your registration prior to us making you an offer. Who knew that this would have offered us the opportunity to bypass the six-month waiting period?

However, I hope you know by now that we would have certainly waited for the noncompete to end and then extended the same offer.

We look forward to seeing you in our Manhattan office on Monday and then in the St. Louis office the following week.

We've made your initial travel accom-
modations, and we will send a car to pick you
up Monday. Until then, have a great weekend, and we look forward to having you join
Parker, Stokes, Addison, and Associates.

Mark Addison
President and Chief Finance Officer
Parker, Stokes, Addison, and Associates

Ava beamed with pride as she read the message. She felt
blessed to have landed such a great opportunity with what
seemed like an exceptional company. There were new projects
to manage and tasks to tackle, but she was up for the challenge.

Feeling a bit sick to her stomach, Ava hoped she wasn't
coming down with the flu before her first day at the new job.
Remembering she hadn't eaten anything substantial yet, Ava
gathered the rest of her office belongings, took a long last look
around, and decided to leave her office at Truman's for the last
time.

She rounded the corner and saw Silvia. "Ms. Beck, I will
be heading out now. A little earlier than anticipated, but I've
squared everything away and am all packed up. If the team
needs me for any reason, please forward their calls," Ava said as
she pushed the elevator key.

"Ms. Stillman, are you sure you don't want to take any of
the cake from your going-away party earlier today? I would be
happy to wrap some up for you. It'll only take a few seconds,"
Silvia said, trying to give Ava the rest of her cake.

"Oh, thank you, but I'm sure the team here would love a
little sugar rush later this afternoon. Besides, it's Friday, and I

had a piece already. It was scrumptious," Ava said, closing her eyes and relieving the taste.

The elevator doors opened, and Ava stepped inside. Turning around to hit the P for parking garage, Ava said, "Have an amazing weekend, Silvia, and remember I'm only a phone call away."

Smiling, Silvia said, "Thank you, Ava. You as well!"

Ava made it down to her car in the parking garage, and she loaded up her box into the trunk of her car. She looked at the six boxes filling up her trunk and back seat but still couldn't believe that today was her last day at Truman—the place she had called home for the past decade.

The day was emotional for Ava, much more so than she had imagined. Her stomach growled as she closed the lid to her trunk. *I better get something to eat,* thought Ava.

Smiling to herself, Ava knew exactly where she wanted to treat herself on her last day—The Bistro. It was the first restaurant that she went to on her very first day at Truman Partners. A bit poetic to start and stop at the same establishment, but the food was delicious.

Ava managed to acquire the same booth by the busy window. She remembered thinking, *What a great way to observe city life.* Although life had not worked out the way she thought, it sure had been a wild ride.

From going up the ranks at Truman to managing multimillion and even billion-dollar deals, I had mastered the art of negotiation, strategy, and relationship management, at least at work, she thought to herself.

The personal side of her life had taken an interesting turn, but nevertheless, she was excited that she and Cal were able to reconnect when she was back with Shelby.

Ava told herself, *I wasn't quite sure how everything would have worked out, but perhaps it was better this way.*

Daydreaming and thinking of what might have been with her and Cal, Ava's meal arrived—a perfectly seared salmon atop a goat cheese, walnut, and dried cranberry salad with a vinaigrette that was famous.

Halfway through her meal, Ava felt sick and rushed to the bathroom. Not understanding why she had thrown up, she began to feel warm and dizzy.

Ava began taking deep breaths to calm herself down and put a paper towel soaked with cold water on her neck.

After a few minutes, she was no longer warm or dizzy, but she wondered if she might have the onset of the flu or perhaps she was anemic.

Feeling well enough to make it back to her table, she quickly grabbed the bill, boxed up her food, and headed toward her car.

Not wanting to be sick for work on Monday, she called her friend Lilly, who was a doctor at a local hospital. "Hi, Lilly, it's Ava! How are you doing?"

"Hi, Ava, I'm well. How are you doing? Big day, I'm sure. Are you up for drinks tonight? I should be off my shift by six or so," Lilly said, excited to see Ava on her last day of work.

"Well, I was actually calling to see if you might be able to see me?"

"Of course. Is everything okay?" Lilly asked, concerned.

"I think I might have food poisoning or coming down with the flu. I don't feel well and thought if I could get antibiotics and stay ahead of it, maybe I won't feel like crap my first week of work," Ava said with a laugh.

"Sure, come on in, and we'll take a look. I can't guarantee that you will need antibiotics, but we can always get you rehydrated, which will help you feel better quicker," Lilly said. "Just come in through the main entrance and check in at the nurses' station. I'll let them know you are coming, and they will notify me when you arrive."

"Aw, you're the best, Lil!" Ava said, happy that she had a plan of action to kick this stomach bug.

After Ava checked in with the nurses' station, she was back with Lilly in no time. "Wow, that was quick," Ava said, surprised.

"Well, Ava, it's all about who you know," Lilly said as they both laughed together. "Okay, let's take a look."

Lilly looked Ava over and checked her symptoms. "Well, you don't have a fever, which would indicate flu along with your other symptoms, and you're not violently ill, so I don't think food poisoning. Why did you think you were sick again, Ava?" Lilly asked, confused.

"My stomach has been upset all day. I got sick almost immediately after eating lunch. Plus, I got really dizzy and warm," Ava said, trying to convince her friend that she wasn't crazy or imagined everything.

"Well, with your mom just having experienced the bouts of dizziness, I can see why you might be concerned. Let's do blood work to run some tests. You are a bit dehydrated, so we'll start you on fluids. Once we have the labs back, we can go from there. But, Ava, I'm sure everything is fine, and you have nothing to worry about," Lilly said as she walked out of the room, closing the curtain for privacy.

Ava thought about calling Shelby to tell her she was in the hospital, but she didn't want to worry her, especially since this was probably just a bug.

It had been nearly three weeks since Shelby came home from the hospital, and she couldn't have been doing better. She was slowly getting back to her normal routines, eating healthier, and experiencing no dizziness.

Keeping her pact with Shelby, Ava had planned to travel to Keokuk next Thursday after she had completed her evaluations at the St. Louis location.

Ava knew Shelby had a follow-up doctor's appointment on Friday, and she wanted to be there with her.

Nearly an hour later, Lilly opened the curtain with a smirk on her face.

"Well, with that smile, I'm guessing I don't have an incurable disease," Ava said, laughing nervously.

"No, Ava, not an incurable disease," Lilly said, trying not to smile. "Just a little bug that with the right treatment, should go away in about seven to eight months."

Confused at first, Ava said, "Wait, what?"

"Ava, you are dizzy, your stomach is upset, and you feel warm because you are about seven to eight weeks pregnant according to your hCG levels," Lilly said with a beaming smile.

"You're going to be a mom, Ava. Congratulations!"

Stunned beyond words, Ava sat there, looking down at her hands. "I can't believe this is happening," Ava said in disbelief.

"Ava, this is a miracle! You told us girls that you didn't think this was possible. Not after you and Cal lost the baby in college," Lilly said, grabbing tissues and handing them to Ava who started to cry.

"I know. I didn't think my body could handle another pregnancy, let alone actually getting pregnant again. You want to know the crazy thing, Lil? It's Cal's baby!" Ava said through the tears.

"Wait, what? Ava, in the couple weeks you've been back and the few girls' nights we've had, you never told us that you and Cal got back together," Lilly said, shocked.

Suddenly, it hit Ava. "Oh no! Lil, I drank when we went out. That's not good. Is the baby okay? Did I hurt my baby?"

The thought that Ava had unintentionally hurt her unborn child sent her into a tailspin of emotion.

Trying to calm her friend down, Lilly told her that they could do an ultrasound to make sure everything was progressing as it should, but seeing how it was so early in the pregnancy, she didn't think it would have been damaging.

As Lilly was setting up the ultrasound next to the bed, she asked, "So why didn't you tell us that you two were back together? That's wonderful news, Ava."

Trying not to cry harder, Ava said, "Well, we were together, and I thought we were going to try and make it work, but then he said he wasn't willing to work it out. He said that getting over me was too difficult the first time, and he didn't want to go through that again. Ultimately, it came down to not wanting to do the back-and-forth to see what came of it. At least that's what he told me."

"Wow! Well, I'm sure that would all change now, especially with a baby in the picture, right? And now you can work from anywhere with the new company. I mean don't get me wrong. I do not want you to leave New York. But to start a family with the man—let's face it—you've always loved and still have your dream job seems like what you've always wanted, Ava," Lilly said, confused why it didn't seem clearer to her friend.

"I agree. It does seem like it would all line up, but do I really want to be with someone who didn't want to try and make it work with just me? Now, I'm going to introduce a new little life into the picture and expect him to just go with it, knowing that he never really wanted to put the effort into the relationship in the first place?" Ava said, trying to be realistic.

Lilly inserted the wand and began searching for the baby's heartbeat. Ava, who had been down that path before, desperately wanted to see the flickering heartbeat.

Last time Ava was in that position, she had Cal by her side. She secretly hoped he was there again, but more importantly, Ava searched the screen for a little flickering sac.

"Lil, I don't see the heartbeat," Ava said, getting emotional. "Did I do something wrong? Did I lose my second chance to be a mom?"

"Ava, stop it. You didn't do anything wrong the first time," Lilly said matter-of-factly. "Just give it a sec and... There it is."

Quickly turning her head, Ava saw the two little flutters coming together over and over again. "Oh, my goodness," Ava said with tears in her eyes. "Is that...is that her heartbeat?"

"Her? Well, I'm not sure about her, but yes, I see a nice, strong heartbeat," Lilly said, smiling and removing the wand.

"So now what, Ava? Are you going to tell Cal?"

Trying to let it all soak in, Ava said, "I'm not sure what's next, but yes, I will eventually need to tell Cal. But first, I need to decide what I want and what is best for my little bug."

They both laughed, but Lilly knew that it would be a difficult decision for Ava. Lilly thought the world of Ava and knew she deserved happiness, especially after everything she had been through in the past few months.

Ava gathered her purse and told Lilly that she would see her later after she got back from Keokuk in a few weeks.

21

The visits in the Manhattan office and St. Louis office went extremely well. Ava listened to what all the employees said, learned where they wanted to be in the new company structure, and planned to lead the company down a successful path.

She had taken copious notes at each departmental meeting and saw a strategic plan on how she could restructure and realign people in various roles that would feed their desire to still be a part of the forward direction of the company while also making the organization run more efficiently.

The last night before Ava planned to drive to Shelby's house, she drafted out an organizational plan and sent it off to Parker, Stokes, and Addison for review.

She reminded them that she would be out of pocket on Friday but would be returning on Monday to the St. Louis office.

Ava's proposal for the presidents laid the restructure and how it would make the progression of the company more efficient, while not having to reassign any employee to a role they were not well suited for or had background knowledge.

The task was daunting, but Ava managed to strategically place each person in a position where they could excel if they wanted.

Once the team approved the proposal, Ava intended to meet with HR in St. Louis on Monday and then the HR team in Manhattan on Tuesday so they could implement.

Ava took the three-hour drive to decide how she was going to tell Shelby and ultimately Cal that she was pregnant.

She secretly wished that she and Cal could be a family, but it was apparent to her that something changed for him after that night. Ava just couldn't figure out what made him want to walk away.

The drive also gave time for Ava to think about what it meant to be pregnant. Before leaving New York, she managed to get in to see her OB-GYN on Saturday.

They performed an official ultrasound and confirmed she was seven weeks and three days pregnant. They could hear a very strong heartbeat at 163 beats per minute.

Ava's doctor told her to start taking prenatal vitamins to help the baby develop, and that she should have a follow-up appointment around twelve weeks.

Of all the timing in the world, Ava couldn't believe that she was pregnant and right in the midst of her new job, but she also felt a warm glow about herself.

It was difficult for Ava to describe, but she was amazed at the miracle of life growing inside her and how it could possibly be.

An article Ava read after she lost her first baby said that it could be extremely challenging, physically and emotionally, to get pregnant again. And if a second pregnancy were to occur and carry to term, the baby would be considered a rainbow baby.

At that moment, Ava looked out her window and saw a rainbow over the mountains. She always thought of her dad when she saw a rainbow.

The day he passed, one appeared out over the lake behind their house. Ever since then, Ava thought, whenever she saw a rainbow, it was her dad watching over her.

Although it wasn't the best way to start a family, Ava couldn't have been more excited to be having a baby. She found herself putting her hand to her stomach and gently rubbing her hand over her belly, saying, "Hi, little bug. Are you having a good day? Mommy can't wait to meet you."

Her heart beat a little faster every time she talked to the baby because she was so excited to meet him or her.

Pulling up to Shelby's house, Ava took a deep breath and turned off the car. She whispered out loud, "You can do this Ava. You can do this!"

"Mom. I'm home," Ava said as she opened the front door.

"In here, dear," Shelby said from the kitchen.

Ava made her way down the foyer and into the kitchen, "Mom, wow, you look great! What are you up to?"

"Well, I was trying to have dinner ready by the time you got here tonight. But you are an hour earlier than I was expecting."

Ava sat her purse on the counter and walked over to Shelby for a hug. "Missed you, Mom," Ava said, a little sad.

"So tell me all about it. How were the office visits? Did you find your plan of action, as you called it, for where everyone would fit?" Shelby said, sounding interested in Ava's past few weeks on the new job.

"It's actually going great! It's different than what I've been doing at Truman, but the people are amazingly sweet. The presidents gave me the flexibility I need to get the job done, along with the support to bring forward my ideas on how we can restructure the two companies as they come together to make them more impactful as they merge together all the pieces."

Ava spoke with such passion that Shelby could see her eyes light up as she continued on about her plan for the company and how she would personally have a hand in its structure.

They sat down for a delicious homemade dinner. Shelby had made her famous shepherd's pie with a fresh green salad and cookie brownie for dessert, all of which were some of Ava's favorite meals.

Finishing her entire plate and dessert, Ava sat back from the table and put her napkin down beside her plate. "Mom, this was amazing. Thank you so much for the meal. Are you ready for your doctor's appointment tomorrow?"

Taking in a breath, Shelby said, "I am. I feel great, and the medicine seems to be working as I haven't been dizzy or fainted since you were last here. It's incredible that Dr. Sophie and Cal reran the bloodwork and tried these new meds. Not sure what would have happened if they hadn't."

"I don't want to even think about it, Mom. I can't imagine you not in my life, especially now," Ava said, looking down.

"What do you mean, kiddo? Especially now? Is something going on with work or Eric? I'd support you with anything you wanted to do, but please God tell me you didn't get back with Eric," Shelby said emphatically.

Laughing, Ava said, "No, Mom. I didn't get back with Eric. Actually, I… I am…" Ava had a more difficult time telling Shelby than she thought.

"Sweetheart, just spit it out. It can't be that bad," Shelby said, extending her hand across the table to Ava.

Ava grabbed her hand, looked up at Shelby, and, without stumbling, said, "Mom, you're going to be a grandmother."

Shelby's eye swelled up with tears and smiled so big. "Oh, Ava, I'm so happy for you. Congratulations! You're going to be a momma," Shelby said, beaming.

"And before you get too nervous, the father is not Eric. It's Cal," Ava said with a little hesitation.

"Ava, as long as you are happy, healthy, and keep my little grandson or granddaughter safe in there," Shelby said, pointing to Ava's stomach, "I'll be just fine."

Shelby was so ecstatic that she leapt out of her chair and engulfed Ava in a hug that lasted forever.

Having a moment to think about Cal being the father, Shelby pushed back from Ava and looked at her confused.

"I didn't realize you two were back together. I mean, I think anyone could see the sparks between you two when you were back here for those few months, but I didn't realize it was official. How come Cal wasn't here when you told me?" Shelby said.

"He actually doesn't know yet. I thought we were going to work it out. You know, be a couple again, but something changed. I was still at Truman Partners when we decided to give it a go, but I'm not sure what happened. I guess he got spooked. He said that he didn't want to go through the hurt of losing me again and didn't want to try and make it work."

"That's an odd response from a man who has swooned over you since grade school. I wonder what caused him to say that. He did seem a little taken aback to see you with Eric out in the garden when we were at the hospital, but I thought it was simply because he wanted to pulverize him like I did," Shelby said with a giggle.

Ava's mind raced, trying to align the timing of everything. She wondered if Cal saw Ava with Eric and thought they were getting back together, which was why he acted that way.

"Oh my goodness! I bet that's why he said that," Ava said out loud as she came to the realization. "But why wouldn't he just ask me? Why would he walk away again? That doesn't make any sense."

"Walk away? What are you talking about? I thought you ended it with Cal so you could study and move to New York?" Shelby said, confused.

"Well, sort of. I gave him an easy way out, and he took it."

Being older, Ava now realized that her breaking it off with Cal was simply her way of getting out of a serious relationship as well, especially after the loss of their pregnancy, which Shelby did not know.

Shelby sat up and cleared the table but turned around and said, "Ava, the past is what it is, and neither of you can change what happened. But anything can happen now. Just go after what your heart wants, and if your heart wants Cal, go get him!"

Ava felt a moment of pure excitement and grabbed her purse. "I think I might just do that."

"Wait, Ava, I didn't mean now," Shelby shrieked as she came back from the kitchen to find Ava had run out the front door.

Ava started her car and headed toward the hospital. She figured if Cal was working rounds, then he would be there; if not, she might be able to see him at Shelby's doctor's appointment tomorrow morning.

When Ava pulled into the parking lot, she saw Cal's truck in the physician's lot. She felt butterflies in her stomach and touched her belly, saying, "Okay, little bug. Let's go tell your daddy that you're coming soon."

Ava walked up to the hospital doors, but before going in, she could see the nurses' station through the glass windows. And there stood Cal. He was filling out what Ava assumed were patient charts.

She began to walk in the doors when an attractive blond nurse approached him, put her hands in his arm, and laid her head down on his shoulder.

Ava didn't really understand what she was seeing. She told herself, *Well, maybe they are just friends.*

But the more she watched their interaction, the more she thought back to what Eric had done to her—all the lying, deceiving, and cheating. Ava couldn't bear to go through that again.

Turning around, she ran to her car in tears and drove back to Shelby's house.

Shelby was sitting in her rocking chair crocheting when Ava came in the door crying. Shelby immediately stood up to comfort Ava and learned what happened with Cal.

"Oh, Mom, it was awful. He was with another woman. A nurse! How stupid was I to think that he would want to be with me again after all this time?" Ava sobbed.

"Ava, sweetheart, first let's calm down. Breath. All this crying and getting upset isn't good for you or the baby. Now, let's take a step back. What nurse are you talking about?" Shelby said in a calm, soothing voice.

"I don't know. A pretty one," Ava said, snarling at Shelby.

"Okay, let's get a bit more descriptive, shall we?" Shelby said, trying to discover who Ava saw.

Ava went on to describe what she saw and how chummy the two seemed to be. Then how it made her think of Eric and what he did with Jackie.

Shelby stroked Ava's hair and said, "Now, Ava, you know Cal is nothing like Eric. You yourself said that you're not a couple. But I do not think what you saw is what you think it is."

"My hunch is that it was Betty-Ann, one of the L and D nurses. She often comes down to the nurses' station to talk with us when the delivery rooms are slow."

Ava started to calm down and take slower breaths, thinking that what she saw might not have been Cal with another woman.

"But, Mom, I know what I saw. She was all over him, and she even kissed him."

"Well, maybe I'm wrong, but there is only one way that you will find out for sure and that is to talk with Cal. You're a momma now, Ava, and that means putting that little one first. I think Cal deserves to know that he has a little one on the way so he can do the same, don't you?"

Shelby asked Ava if she wanted some hot tea, but Ava shook her head and sat in silence, thinking about what Shelby had said.

After a little while, they both decided to go to bed and rest before her doctor's appointment tomorrow.

22

The next morning, Ava was more composed and knew how she was going to tell Cal, but first she wanted to know where they stood and why he walked away from them.

At the doctor's appointment, Shelby met with Dr. Sophie, who gave a glowing review of how well Shelby was doing.

Dr. Sophie even said for Shelby not to come back for another eight weeks. Ava was proud of her mother for how far she had come in what seemed like such a short time.

On their way out of the doctor's office, Ava and Shelby ran into Cal, who was headed into work.

"Ava," Cal said, surprised to see her back in town. "What are you doing here? I thought you went back to New York."

Not to be rude, Cal also greeted Shelby but was more confused as to why Ava was not in New York.

"Hi, Cal," Ava said softly. Shelby made pleasantries and then headed off to the car.

"I came back to go with Mom to her appointment. How are you?" Ava asked genuinely.

"I'm fine. And you?" Cal asked rather short.

Ava brushed her hand over her stomach, saying, "I'm great. I actually started a new job that offers me more flexibility so I can be here for Mom more often."

"Wow," Cal said, surprised. "That's great. I'm happy for you, Ava. It's as if you're glowing or something. You seem really happy."

"I am. Thank you. And you seem good as well. I stopped by the hospital last night, but you seemed busy, so I didn't want to bother you," Ava said, almost gathering up the courage to tell him about the baby when Cal interrupted her and said he was late for an appointment.

"Oh, okay. Well, maybe we can talk later?" Ava said as she walked back to the car.

"Sure thing!" Cal yelled as he entered the doctor's office suite.

Getting into the driver's side of the car, Shelby asked Ava how Cal took the news.

"I didn't have a chance to tell him. He said he had to run to an appointment."

"It's not going to be easy, sweetheart, but you have to tell him," Shelby said as she put her hand on Ava's shoulder.

"I know, Mom. I know," Ava said softly, turning on the car and driving back to the house.

When they arrived at their home, Ava asked if Shelby would be okay by herself for an hour or so.

Inquiring where she was going, Ava told her to see her father.

"I'll be fine, dear. All good results from the doctor, and I'm feeling great. Say hello to your dad for me, and tell him that I love him," Shelby said with a sweet smile.

"Will do, Mom." And with that, Ava drove away toward Calvary Cemetery about a half hour away from their house.

Ava could always talk to her dad about anything, regardless of how difficult, and it was in that moment that Ava wished he was still around to tell him he was going to be a grandpa.

The next best thing she could think of was to visit his grave. She hadn't been there in a while, so it seemed fitting.

Pulling up to the entrance, she remembered his ashes were buried under the large oak tree on the very last row. No matter how many storms came through their little town, that oak tree stood tall and strong.

She opened the car door and sauntered up to his headstone. "Hi, Daddy."

Ava knelt down in front of his grave. "I miss you so much. Mom sends her love. She misses you so much, Dad. I wish you were still here. I have some big news to tell you, although you probably already know. I'm going to have a baby! But I'm guessing you may have had a hand in picking this little bug for me," Ava said, touching her belly and laughing.

As a tear started to fall, Ava sobbed, "Daddy, I'm not sure what to do. How do I tell the man who I've always loved that I'm carrying his baby when I know he doesn't want to be with me? I don't want to force him into something and then have him resent me for it. God, I wish you were here right now. You'd probably say something like, 'Ava, what do you want? Figure that out and go after it. Listen to your heart, and if he's smart, he'll come running.'"

Ava chuckled as she thought about what her father would tell her in that moment.

Just then the wind started to pick up and the sun pierced through the oak tree, scattering sunlight across John's headstone.

The leaves on the branches began rustling, and the birds flew out of the tree as if they knew a storm was on the way.

As Ava followed the bird's flight, she saw a truck turning on to the last lane in the cemetery. Ava took a closer look, and it looked like Cal's truck.

Not understanding if it was really Cal or not, Ava stayed knelt down. The truck stopped, and Cal jumped out of the cab.

"Cal?" Ava said. "What are you doing here?"

Cal slowly walked over to Ava, saying, "Ava, it took me a couple of minutes, but I remember the last time I saw you that happy. With that glow about you."

Ava looked at Cal and couldn't believe he already knew, and she didn't even have to tell him. Her heart began pounding with excitement.

"I just wanted to tell you in person, congratulations and that I'm happy for you. Even if that means we're not together. And you and Eric are going to start a family together. I just—"

Ava cut Cal off before he went any further. "Wait, what? Me and Eric? What are you talking about? He and I were never back together."

"I'm sorry, what? At the hospital, I saw you two together, and it looked like you were back together. Then you darted back to New York," Cal said, confused.

"Yes, Eric did come here hoping to patch things up, but that was never going to happen. Besides what do you care if I'm with anyone? You looked pretty chummy with your nurse friend the other night."

Cal thought back to what happened, and the only thing he could think of was Betty-Ann. "Wait, do you mean Betty-Ann? She might be friendly as can be, but I'm pretty sure her wife would have something to say if she were attracted to men."

Ava seemed relieved that Cal wasn't seeing the nurse she saw him with the other night. "Oh, I didn't realize."

Trying to piece everything together, Ava said, "So the reason you told me you didn't want to work things out when I lived in New York was because you thought I got back with Eric?"

"Yes!" Cal said emphatically. "Ava, I've only ever wanted you to be happy. And if that's not with me, then so be it, but I wasn't going to sit back and let you stomp all over me again."

Cal dropped to his knees beside Ava, and in a soft, husky voice said, "But if you're telling me that you want me. Baby, I'll move mountains to be with you. I'll move to New York if that's what it takes. Just say you want us and make me the happiest man in the world. And I promise, I'll spend the rest of my days committed to you and loving only you."

Ava started to cry at the thought Cal wanted to be with her. Overcome with emotion, she reached for his face and drew him into hers. She kissed him with so much passion, and he matched her right back.

They parted and Cal rubbed Ava's tears away with his hand.

"So now that we have that squared away, am I right? Are you...pregnant?" Cal said anxiously.

Ava nodded, yes.

Cal brought Ava's forehead to his and then kissed her. "We will be an amazing family. I promise you to raise him or her like they were my own. I will love—"

Ava raised her hand over Cal's mouth and said, "Cal, the baby is yours."

With water filling up in his eyes, he sat on the ground. "I'm going to be a dad. Really? After what happened last time, I never thought this would be possible. I can't believe this is happening," Cal said, putting his hands over his head.

"Yeah, you're telling me," Ava said, sitting down herself. "Try starting a new job and having your friend tell you you're pregnant when you think its food poisoning or the flu."

They both laughed.

Cal took Ava's hand and without hesitation asked, "Will you marry me, Ava? Will you make me the happiest man from here until the end of time?"

Ava smiled. "Yes, yes, a thousand times yes."

Cal stood up and twirled Ava around, hugging her so tight.

"I can't believe it. After all this time, we can finally be husband and wife. It's our second chance."

Getting her footing on the ground, Ava pushed the hair out of Cal's eyes and said, "Home is wherever we are together, and I promise today, I will love you more than I did yesterday but not as much as I will tomorrow."

Hearing his own words repeated back to him, Cal was beaming with happiness.

As they walked back to their cars, Ava turned back to her father's grave, saying, "Thanks, Dad. You always knew how to make things better. Love you."

23

Seven months later

"Cal, honey, if you don't hurry, you're going to be late for work!" Ava shouted from the breakfast nook.

Barreling down the stairs, Cal looked in the hallway mirror to finish buttoning his shirt. "I know. I know. I should have gotten up earlier. Then we could have had breakfast together," Cal retorted as he turned the corner into the kitchen.

"Well, now, you'll just have to sit for five minutes and scarf down these eggs and bacon I made for you before you head off to work," Ava said with a smart-alecky smile.

"Yes, dear," Cal said jokingly.

As Cal sat down for breakfast, he asked Ava what she had planned for today. "Well, I have a meeting with Addison to discuss our new reporting structure and efficiency ratio with the new positions I recommended for the St. Louis production team. Then I have another big meeting this afternoon with

Parker, Stokes, and Addison to discuss who will cover the pressing projects during my maternity leave."

Cal looked at Ava with pride. "You never cease to amaze me. You're almost ready to pop, and you are still cracking the whip at work."

Ava smiled. "I know. I can definitely get used to this remoting from home thing."

Cal, taking his dishes to the sink, asked Ava if she had plans to meet up with Shelby for lunch today since they only lived ten minutes away from each other.

"Yes, I have a break from twelve thirty to two, so Mom's going to come over here with lunch."

"Okay, remember you have to eat to maintain your strength for you and our little one," Cal said as he touched Ava's growing belly. Ava shook her head as she had heard Cal's protective guidance all throughout her pregnancy.

He leaned down to kiss her stomach, and the baby kicked his hand. "Well, good morning to you too," Cal said giddily.

Since Cal and Ava wanted to be surprised with the baby's gender, they decided not to learn the sex of the baby beforehand.

Grabbing his bag and kissing Ava goodbye, Cal said, "Call me if you need anything."

"Will do, husband. Now get going to work or you'll be late," Ava said as she pulled him in for one more kiss.

"Remember, I'm at the hospital today!" Cal shouted as he headed out the back door.

Ava finished breakfast and got ready for the day.

She finished up her meeting with Addison and began prepping for her afternoon meeting with the team to determine coverage while she was out with the baby.

Shelby showed up right on time with lunch, and they ate quickly before Ava had to run to her next meeting. But before

Shelby left, she showed Ava some of the clothes she brought over for the baby.

"Now, this one is if it's a boy, and this one is if it's a girl," Shelby said as she laid out two beautifully hand-stitched, zip-up onesies.

"Oh, Mom, these are amazing. Did you make them?" Ava said, running her hands over the tiny outfits.

"Well, sort of. I found a matching pair with a blue-and-pink design, and then I sewed on the 'Heaven Sent with Love' saying across the chest. Just a little piece of grandma for the little one to have when he or she arrives," Shelby said with a big smile.

"I love it. Thank you," Ava said. "We will make sure to wash them so both can go in our hospital bag."

Ava saw Shelby to the front door and got back to work. After nearly two hours of meeting with the team, Ava had successfully prepared for her three months of maternity leave.

Feeling a huge weight lifted off her shoulders, Ava decided to take a break and grab a snack.

She stood up and felt a leaky burst. Not knowing if something was wrong with the baby, Ava immediately went to the bathroom to see if she was bleeding.

Grabbing her phone on the way, she got to the bathroom, only to find that it was water that wouldn't stop trickling out. *Oh, wow. It's happening. My water broke.*

Ava tried calling Cal right away, but it went straight to voice mail. "Oh, of course, he would be in a dead cell spot in the hospital. Are you kidding me?"

Continuing to try Cal's cell, Ava made it upstairs to their bedroom and finished packing the hospital bag.

She grabbed the two outfits, which her mother dropped off earlier that day, from the dryer and threw them into the bag.

Just as Ava was getting ready to call Shelby, Cal's name appeared on Ava's cell phone. "Oh, thank goodness," Ava said as calmly as she could.

"Ava, what's wrong? Is the baby okay? Are you okay?" Cal said in a panic.

Semi-laughing, Ava said, "We're fine, but I'm pretty sure my water broke, and we need to get to the hospital."

"I'm on my way. Be there in fifteen minutes."

Cal arrived just as Ava finished getting the hospital bags downstairs by the door.

He rushed in to find Ava as calm as could be, just holding her belly with a smile on her face.

"You ready to meet your son or daughter, Dr. Michaels?"

"Oh, you have no idea, Mrs. Michaels," Cal said as he rushed to Ava's side, kissing her sweetly.

* * *

After twenty-three hours of labor, Cal stepped out from the delivery room and found Shelby patiently waiting. "Shelby, would like to come meet your granddaughter?"

Shelby's eyes filled with water. "Yes, please! A baby girl. I should have known she'd be strong like her momma."

"Mom and baby are doing great!" Cal said with pride.

Cal led Shelby back to the recovery room where Ava was waiting with the baby.

When Shelby entered the room, she saw the tiniest, most precious baby she had ever seen lying in Ava's arms.

"Mom, we'd like you to meet Ashley J Michaels," Ava said as she handed the baby to Shelby.

"Oh, you kids did well. She is simply amazing. So beautiful and precious. Ava, she has your eyes and strength. Watch out, world," Shelby said with a chuckle.

Shelby looked down at her granddaughter and was in awe at the incredible love she had for this little baby. "Ava, how are you doing?"

"I'm on cloud nine, Mom," Ava said, taking the baby back.

Shelby leaned in to kiss Ashley on the top of her head. "Nice to meet you, Ashley J. I am your grandma, and I love you more than you'll ever know."

After a few moments, Shelby asked Cal and Ava what the J stood for in Ashley's name, and Ava said, "It's so she can have a little bit of Dad with her wherever she goes. He may not be here to meet her, but we will tell her all about him so it's as if she's always known him."

Shelby was taken aback and said, "That's a lovely sentiment, Ava. Your dad would be proud."

They all gathered around the baby and marveled at the new little life that had been brought into the world.

Later that evening, when Cal had stepped out to grab a coffee from the cafeteria and Shelby had gone home, Ava lifted her knees and propped Ashley against her legs.

Ashley was still used to being in the womb that her legs bent up to her chest. Ava snuggled her in the blanket and made sure she was warm.

"Ashely, I promise you that I will love you unconditionally. Wherever you go, I will be in your heart because you are a piece of me and I am a piece of you. I prayed for you, my sweet girl. I prayed that you would be strong and healthy. And here you are. This amazing and beautiful little person. I will protect you and show you wrong from right."

Cal, returning from the cafeteria, heard Ava talking and stopped outside the room as to not interrupt but still able to hear.

He leaned up against the doorframe and watched as his wife vowed to their new daughter to give her the world, vowed to show her that anything is possible, and told her that she would know more love than she could possibly imagine.

As Ava brought Ashley to her chest to fall asleep, she saw Cal standing in the door. "Hey, you."

"Hey," Cal said, putting down the drinks he got for Ava and himself. "I knew it."

"Knew what?" Ava said with curiosity.

"That you would be the most amazing mother. You're a natural," Cal said, looking down at Ashley fast asleep. "Look at that. She already loves you more than you can imagine."

"Cal, thank you for giving me my second chance to become a mom," Ava said with a heart full of love.

With that, Cal took Ava's hand and kissed it gently. "Thank you for making me the happiest man in the world and a dad to our wonderful daughter. You are simply incredible, and I'm proud to call you my wife."

They both looked at each other with love in their hearts and then looked at the love they both made, thinking how could life get any better than that moment.

About the Author

A. S. McConnell, author of *Second Chances*, strives to give her audience an experience they will remember long after they have left her novels. From moments of gumption and drive to fleeting desires that turn to passion, McConnell's words inspire an emotional connection to the characters.

> My aspiration with any novel is to establish a bond with the reader so they can take the journey alongside the characters. For me, to elicit an emotional response from your audience is amazing, but to provide an experience—that is the ultimate honor.
>
> —A. S. McConnell

McConnell established roots in the Washington, DC area but will always be a Floridian at heart. Her passions reside in the creative realm from photography, event planning, graphic design, and traveling on adventures with her family. McConnell continues to write while raising amazing children who light up her world.

CPSIA information can be obtained
at www.ICGtesting.com
Printed in the USA
FSHW012206191219
65300FS